Tear

A Seaside Novel #1

by

RACHEL VAN DYKEN

Tear
by Rachel Van Dyken

TEAR

ISBN 13: 978-1495224133
ISBN: 1495224139
Cover Art Designed by P.S. Cover Design

Chapter One

It was a normal day in my normal life, and it should have been everything I've come to expect in the sleepy town of Seaside, Oregon.

I'd wake up, brush my teeth, careful to sing Happy Birthday at least three times before I stopped. I was paranoid like that. I often had dreams my teeth would fall out. A friend once told me that meant someone was going to die in your family.

If only.

I know that sounds harsh, but then at least something beside the norm would happen to me. Not that I was insane enough to start wishing for family members to keel over. Maybe it was all this teenage angst. At eighteen, I was just finishing out my senior year of high school.

To say I could not wait to go to college would be the understatement of the century.

I had a calendar with giant red x marks over each day.

Nine months.

That's all I had. And then I was free.

Free of this boring oh so normal place, and free for

change to happen. Crap, even getting my hair dyed a different color than the golden blonde it was would be enough change for me.

But my mom hated artificial anything.

What can I say? We live in Oregon. We hug trees and all that.

I spit the last bit of toothpaste into the sink and looked into the mirror.

"Ugh." I cringed at my reflection. Why couldn't my eyes have been anything but brown?

I blamed my parents.

Their boring genes became my boring genes and voila, here I am.

I slipped on a pair of faded skinny jeans, threw on a pair of tennis shoes and a tight- fitting V-neck Henley. It wasn't that cold outside yet but everyone knew that the weather in Seaside could turn from gorgeous to disastrous within minutes.

I walked into the bathroom and pinched my cheeks. My parents wouldn't let me wear makeup.

I know, weird.

Eighteen and I'd never kissed a boy, never worn makeup, and I drove a semi-new pickup to school.

My only saving grace was that I was actually one of the cooler kids at school. I wasn't sure if that was a positive mark in my favor or another way of explaining just how lame Seaside was.

I put on some lip balm and ran downstairs. I needed to stop acting so moody or my mom would think I was on drugs. Usually, I'm a very happy go lucky girl, but last night had been another rough one.

I had that stupid dream again about the boy with blonde hair. A boy I've never seen before in my life. He drove up to the school and proclaimed his love for me.

I was wearing makeup.

A killer dress.

Oh yeah, and he kissed me.

I always dreamed like that. The dream only occurred once a month and it was always different. My psychiatrist mom would say I was projecting, or possibly suffering from some sort of delusion.

Which I probably was.

However, I thought it was just another sign that I needed to lay off the double mochas and late night TV. You can only watch *One Tree Hill* so many times before you begin to think Chad Michael Murray is actually going to show up at your house one day and proclaim undying love.

I ducked into the kitchen, grabbed my slick rain jacket, put a banana in my backpack, and took a bite out of an apple.

"Mom!"

No answer.

I sighed. "Mom! I'm leaving for school!"

Still no answer.

With patience I knew I didn't possess I screamed her name a third time and waited for her to emerge from her study.

Sure enough after three minutes the door to her study opened. Her glasses were slightly tilted on her face as if she put them on in a rush, her hair in a messy bun. She gave me a cheeky grin and shrugged.

That was good old mom. Her slight build just made her look that much more innocent.

"Sorry, Hon, late night client. Do you need money for lunch?"

"Nope. I still have some from yesterday." I shoved my hands in my pockets and stared into the space right above her head so she would think I was looking at her and paying attention, when really I just wanted to get to school.

"Oh, alright. Well, have a good day."

"Yup." I was already turning on my heel to walk out the

door.

Always the same.

She always fell asleep in her office. There was always some depressed client in this tiny town that wanted to kill themselves. Needless to say, she never needed more work. I blamed the dreary Oregon weather and my mom's inability to say no to anyone. Even me. It sounded like every girl's dream. A parent that said yes all the time?

It wasn't a dream.

She was more of a… I don't know, maybe a roommate? My dad wasn't any better. He was a surgeon. I hardly saw him, but when I did, he usually missed mom so much it was hard to get a word in edgewise.

They were brilliant and would often hoie up in her office with a bottle of wine and talk philosophy.

The idea of drinking wine and talking philosophy literally made my stomach ache. I'd rather watch Reality TV all night while eating sardines.

Sometimes I think they wished I hadn't been born. It wasn't that they didn't love me. I knew I had their love. They just seemed happier without me.

It sucks, but at least I knew what to expect. If you know what to expect you never really get let down. That's what I chanted the entire way to the truck.

I threw in my messenger bag and slammed the door.

The drive to school was short. I had a pretty awesome view of the ocean on the way, too. It helped that my parents lived in a legitimate Better Homes and Gardens beach house.

As I drove into the parking lot, an involuntary shiver ran down my spine.

Weird.

I bit my lip and turned off the ignition.

I don't know how long I sat there, five minutes maybe, and then someone was banging on my window.

"Nat! What the heck? Where have you been?"

My best friend, though I hated to claim her at times considering she had the tendency to be neurotic and slightly irritating, banged on the window again. "The meeting? Did you forget?"

Crap.

I pushed open the door and hopped out. "Sorry, Alesha. I totally spaced it."

She folded her arms across her chest and scowled. "What's up with you lately? We only have thirty days until the dance and Homecoming has to be the best! I mean it's like one of our final hoorays!"

"I think you mean hoorah."

"Whatever." She blinked several times, trying to clear the clumps from her heavy mascara, and threw her bag over her shoulder. "All I'm saying is we need your help. Think you can float out of la la land and make it to the meeting after school?"

"Yes?" I said it as more of a question then flashed her a smile. "Yes, Alesha. I promise I'll make it and I'll do wonderful things with the decorations. Great theme by the way."

"What is it?"

"Life's a Beach?" I guessed.

"Lucky guess…" she muttered then stormed off.

I exhaled and again a prickling awareness washed over my skin. Seriously, I needed to get more sleep. The bell rang. I trudged to my first class not really paying attention to anyone around me which was just a bad choice period. I mean, I'm a teenager. We're clumsy and all that.

Needless to say, I tripped. My messenger bag went flying out of my hands and my books spewed out of my bag like they were angry they were there in the first place.

"Crap." I knelt down and reached for my Poli-Sci book just as another hand brushed mine.

Chills spread throughout my entire body. Alarmed, I pulled back and looked up, straight into the greenest eyes I've ever seen.

Period.

I'm sure my mouth dropped open, because that's the typical girl response when she sees someone so breathtakingly handsome all she really wants to do is curse and then pinch herself to make sure she isn't dreaming.

I felt my skin heat as he wordlessly passed me my book, and then held out his hand to help me up.

I took it, mainly because I was in such shock I didn't know what else to do.

And just as I was about to speak, or exhale, or do anything that would prove to this very beautiful boy that I was in fact a human and not a robot, someone walked up beside him and scowled.

"Knocking girls on their knees already hmm, Alec?"

It was like looking at the sun and moon at the same time. Alec had messy black hair and green eyes. His chin was pronounced, his jaw had a five o'clock shadow on it. No way was this guy a teenager. The boy next to him stretched out his hand and grinned, revealing perfectly straight white teeth. His hair was blonde and curly, his skin the perfect tan, as if he just spent the last few weeks on vacation in Hawaii. His dimples were so deep you could tell he smiled a lot, whereas the other guy, Alec, hadn't said a word. Nor had he smiled. Not once.

"Um..." I took the guy's hand. "He didn't knock me down, he was helping me. I tripped and…" Why the heck was I defending myself like some guilty prisoner?

"No worries." The guy shrugged. "Demetri. And your name?"

"Natalee," I said slowly. "But everyone just calls me Nat. Nice to meet you… both."

Demetri shrugged. "Yeah, well, we're new in town, so I'm sure you'll be seeing more of us."

There was something vaguely familiar about both of them, but I couldn't put my finger on it. Again, it's probably all that late night television watching. No way do I actually know two guys this hot.

I stole a look at Alec. He seemed to be flexing every muscle in his body, almost like he wanted to punch me, or eat me, or maybe just kill me with his bare hands.

Great start to a day.

At least it wouldn't be boring.

"Right, um, like I said, nice meeting you. I'll just..." I didn't finish the sentence, instead I just walked as fast as my legs could take me to my first class praying the whole time that my butt looked good in my jeans and that I had remembered to put on deodorant.

"Nat!" Evan jumped out of his seat and plowed toward me. "Where were you this morning? We waited, but then, you know I got hungry and... well, you weren't there."

I rolled my eyes. "Evan, when are you not hungry? And I totally forgot, sorry."

He shrugged. "No apologies necessary. I just hate having to be the only sane one in that estrogen fest."

I smirked. "Right. You just hate being surrounded by beautiful women."

"It makes it hard for me to eat."

"Why is that?" I took my seat and grinned.

"Well..." he leaned forward. "I can't just maul my food with all those pretty girls watching, and I'm pretty sure eating anything in front of chicks who use laxatives as an appetizer is a quick way to get shot in the face."

"Ah, this is true. Here." I reached into my backpack and took out the banana I had snatched from the counter earlier. "My peace offering."

"Thank God."

"Boys. Give them food and they're putty in your hands."

Evan peeled the banana and took a huge bite. "Please. Any guy would be putty in your hands, Nat. You're freaking hot."

I rolled my eyes, as I did whenever I got a compliment, and was relieved when the teacher told us to take our seats.

"Now, as you all know, this school is part of an exchange student program with other schools around the world." Mr. Meservy cleared his throat and continued, "Because of this program—Evan! Throw that banana peel elsewhere, perhaps the trash can? Not the floor, or I'm going to make you scrub it with a toothbrush."

Evan threw up his hands and made a giant show of throwing the banana into the trash can and returned to his seat. The chair squeaking against the floor.

"You may continue, sir." Evan saluted and winked.

I rolled my eyes and turned back around to face Mr. Meservy. He wasn't my favorite teacher, probably because he was freakishly young and reminded me somewhat of my dad. Weird comparison, I know. In all honesty he looked exactly like pictures of my father when he was young. I only know this because upon seeing him for the first time my mom nearly had a heart attack.

But that's beside the point. Teachers aren't supposed to be only a few years older than students. It's just not right. He had to fight twice as hard to earn the respect due than all the rest of the teachers, even though he was three times as good and brilliant to match.

Mr. Meservy shook his head. "As I was saying..." He gave Evan a pointed glare. "Our school is part of an exchange program, and although we've never had any students utilize this wonderful opportunity, there are two students originally from British Columbia that have taken our school up on this offer."

Two students? Were those the boys I saw this morning? Were they brothers or just friends? They looked like polar opposites. I bit my lip and began tapping my pen against my desk.

"Let's all give them a warm welcome, and please try to be

civil, people. We don't want to scare them into thinking Seaside is filled with druggies and gang bangers." You'd think Mr. Meservy was welcoming the president or something with all the warnings he was giving us, but then again, nothing exciting ever happened here so it kind of made sense.

A sudden knock at the door interrupted his speech.

Every head in the room turned.

The two guys from the hallway walked in. Alec, the brooding one, looked like he'd rather be run over with a car then be in the classroom. And Demetri had his perma-smile pasted across his mouth as if it was the most fun he'd had in years.

"Welcome, welcome." Okay why was Mr. Meservy bowing to them? He clasped his hands in front of him as if he was in the presence of George Clooney and bowed. Yes, our very lame teacher from Seaside, Oregon just bowed to the exchange students. I could have died.

Shocked, I could only watch as Demetri smirked in my direction then returned Mr. Meservy's bow with one of his own. Alec, however, was motionless. His eyes seemed to darken even more as he looked at every person in the room but me. I know because I was waiting for it. Stupid, but I wanted him to look at me. And again, I blame TV. I liked his brooding attitude even though I knew it was just a sign of his immaturity and lack of personality. I couldn't help it.

Demetri winked at me then looked at Mr. Meservy and pumped his hand. "Thank you so much for the warm welcome. I also don't think I've been on the receiving end of a bow since I played Prince Charming in first grade."

Mr. Meservy blushed to the roots of his hair, probably just now realizing that yes, he had indeed bowed to the Canadians. "Well…" He cleared his throat. "Again, welcome to Seaside High."

Demetri nodded and made his way to the back of the class. Alec trailed behind, but not before stopping at my desk.

Our eyes met, and I couldn't pull my gaze away. He was staring through me, uncomfortably so. I opened my mouth to speak but wasn't really sure what to say. Finally, after what was most likely an awkward silence for everyone else in the room but us, Alec spoke.

"I think you dropped this." He placed a pink pen on my desk and continued to his seat in the back. My heart thumped wildly in my chest. Mouth still hanging slightly ajar, I quickly clenched the pen and willed myself to look back at the front of the room.

It was as if nobody had seen the intense exchange between us.

Except five minutes later, I realized I was still clenching the pen and hadn't yet opened my book. It was like I had spaced out or something.

"Geez, Nat, it's just a pen," Evan mumbled behind me. I laughed right along with him even though my heart was still hammering in my chest. The two new kids were gorgeous, that much was obvious, but a small part of me seemed to find them familiar. As if I'd seen them before?

I stole a peek behind me, irritated that Evan tried to block my view. Alec looked away but Demetri flashed me another heart-stopping smile.

And then it hit me.

I knew exactly who those boys were.

Unfortunately, my realization came at the same time as every other girl in the classroom.

The whispering grew louder and then some of the girls shrieked. I looked back at Evan who seemed to be slowly trying to figure out the same thing. He looked at me, then back at the boys, then back at me.

I rolled my eyes and pulled out my phone careful not to let my teacher see. I was so not going to give him ten dollars just because my friend was painfully disconnected from the world enough not to know who those guys were.

I searched AD2 on my phone and held it up to Evan.

"Holy sh— I mean, crap."

Nobody ever said boys were intelligent, or tactful for that matter.

"Those are the dudes from AD2!" He did a fist pump and turned around to give them both a head nod which apparently in boy world meant, "What's up, you're cool, let's hang."

Because he got two very cool-looking head nods back. I rolled my eyes, a little disappointed that my fantasy had ended just as fast as it had begun. The day was no longer boring, but now I knew without a doubt that Alec would not be smoldering in my direction, and Demetri was fortunate enough to be the type of guy that had every STD listed and probably some of them that weren't. The guy was known for his conquests. TMZ followed them everywhere, which begged the question — what the heck were they doing in Seaside?

I scrolled through the pages on my phone trying to find any sort of rumor as to why they were going to school rather than touring or whoring around.

"Miss Murray, your phone." Mr. Meservy held out his hand. Irritated, I slapped it into his hand, but not before clicking the top of it so he'd have to use a password to get in.

"Anyone else want to tempt fate today?" Mr. Meservy looked around the room challenging more students to pull out their phones.

Someone made a choking noise behind me, and suddenly Alec was at the side of my desk. "Um, actually that's my phone. She was probably confused which is why it was out on her desk."

Mr. Meservy rolled his eyes. "Fine, I'll play. And how would she have your phone?"

"She tripped." Alec shrugged giving a cool smile to the teacher. I shivered when his hand gently touched my shoulder. "Her books and phone fell out of her bag and then the bell rang. I helped her grab her stuff, but had to set my phone down on the floor to do so. Simple mistake."

Even I believed him, and I knew it was a bald-faced lie.

"Besides..." Alec leaned his tanned hands against my desk and smirked. "We all know how many times my phone goes off. It was probably burning up in her hand."

At this the entire class began chuckling, because really it had to be true. The guy was a celebrity. Grown women wanted to rape him. Naturally, his phone would be blowing up the cellular universe.

"Fine, Alec, you'll get your phone back at the end of class."

Alec turned his back to Mr. Meservy making me want to gasp. You didn't turn your back on teachers. Clearly I was sheltered.

"Here's your phone, Nat." His smile disappeared. He handed me the iPhone 5, slipping it into my hand before walking back to his desk. It felt sleek in my hands, and insanely more masculine then my sad little free phone with its pink cover.

"Thanks," I mumbled.

I now had two things he had touched and I was ready to fall out of my seat. Seriously. Must. Stop. Watching. TV!

Chapter Two

By lunchtime, word had spread and it was nearly impossible to see Alec and Demetri without a swarm of people stalking them down the hallways. It made me wonder why they chose Seaside of all places. Granted, we were on the Oregon coast — far away from their homeland of Canada, and nowhere near L.A., but still. We had the Internet. We had phones. They were in no way invisible to our sleepy town. It was only a matter of time before they high-tailed it out of here. I mean, they didn't even have body guards!

With a sigh, I fished out my lunch money from my back pocket and looked at the choices of the day.

Tacos or a salad.

Or, I gave a mischievous smile, taco salad. I quickly made my little concoction and grinned even brighter.

"I must say..." A deep voice said from behind me. "I've never seen a girl get so excited over a taco salad."

"Well," I turned to face Demetri, of course it would be Demetri. "I like food. And I think I get a gold star for being creative."

He laughed and leaned in closer his golden hair falling

gracefully across his forehead. "Think you can make me one too?"

I put one hand on my hip. "That depends. Are you asking me so you don't have to make your own, or are you just wanting an excuse to talk to me?"

"Both."

I laughed. "Fair enough. But be warned, perfection doesn't often happen twice in a row."

He smirked and stood next to me as I made him a similar salad. "So, where are all your admirers?"

"With Alec." He nodded his head toward the other side of the cafeteria were Alec was holding court with at least fifty people. His face was as handsome and stern as ever.

"Does he smile, like ever?"

Demetri shook his head, a bright grin creased his lips. "He smiled at you, didn't he?"

"That was a smile?" I handed him his tray. "I thought it was a grimace. Easy to confuse the two on his face."

"Don't let him hear you say that. He may just fall in love with you if you tease him."

"No danger of any guy falling in love, no worries." I kept my head down so I wouldn't have to look at his gorgeous face and walked away, but felt his hand touch my arm.

"Hey, where are you going?"

"To eat, like normal people. It is lunch time and we only get fifteen minutes."

"Sit with me." His blue eyes sparkled, and his dimples seemed even more pronounced as his smile spread even wider across his face. Stupid rock star.

"Um, no thanks," I said as politely as I could.

His smile faded. I continued walking to my usual table, when I felt a hand on my arm again. "No thanks?"

Demetri sure was persistent, but I didn't want to be a part of his harem. "Let me guess, you've never faced rejection before."

He looked a little less confident as he shuffled his feet, his eyebrows drew together. "No, um, not really."

"There's a first for everything, Demetri. Enjoy your salad." I patted him on the shoulder and continued walking in a straight line even though my legs were wobbly. Why the heck did I just turn down a lunch date with the hottest guy I've ever seen?

I turned back around to see if he was following me. Big shock there, he was surrounded by at least twenty girls, each of them touching his arm or shoulder, even his butt. Disgusting. And that was the reason I wasn't sitting with him. I wasn't them. I would never be that girl.

I blew my hair from my face and plopped into my chair. Evan gave me a confused look. "Did he just ask you to eat with him?"

"Maybe."

"Maybe?" Evan repeated. "Are you high?"

"No," I said, as I opened my juice. "I just didn't want to eat with him."

"Right. And I don't want to get laid by Cameron Diaz."

I narrowed my eyes. "Does everything always have to be about sex?"

"Yes." Evan gave me a serious look before taking a huge bite of his sandwich.

There was officially no hope for the male species.

The bell rang a few minutes later, meaning I only got to enjoy part of my salad. I rushed to my next class. Just as I was rounding the corner, a guy bolted out of the classroom door slamming me against the locker and sending me sailing to the ground. For the second time that day my eyes came into contact with expensive boots.

I was literally my own teenage soap opera.

"I promise I'm not doing this on purpose," I said as I pushed myself to my knees and gathered my books, stuffing them into my bag.

Alec leaned down and shook his head. "You sure about that?" His mouth curved upward into a smirk.

I felt my nostrils flare. "Yeah, I promise. Plus, it's not like I trip in order to get attention. That's the last thing I want."

Alec grabbed my bag and handed it to me. "Believe me, you're the center of attention whether you trip or merely walk down the hall. Have a good day, Nat." His hooded green eyes seemed to mock me as he looked me up and down then walked in the other direction. So what if watched the way his muscles stretched underneath his T-shirt?

I sighed and shook my head.

"Really Nat?" Evan whispered over my ear.

"Crap!" I jumped. "Don't scare me like that!"

"Scare you?" Evan put his arm on my shoulder and directed me toward class. "I was standing behind you for like two minutes saying your name before I whispered in your ear. Geez, what's the big deal about those guys? So they're like rock stars. Who cares? They still shit."

I burst out laughing. "Thanks, Evan. Your eloquence and wisdom is always so refreshing."

His chest puffed up as he pushed me teasingly into class. "It's what I do."

The day progressed slowly. I almost believed everything was normal. I walked to my locker and forced it open. It was only Monday and I had enough homework to officially keep me locked in my bedroom all night.

"So, what are you doing tonight?" I knew his voice by heart now. It was deep, sexy, and always had some sort of smug inflection. Maybe it was my imagination, but it seemed like his words always took longer to pronounce than a normal person's.

"Homework." I slammed my locker door shut and gave him a smile. "And you?"

"Whitney."

"Huh?"

Demetri gave me a shameless grin and burst out laughing as I felt my face flush red. "I'm kidding, girl. You really need to get out more."

Preaching to the choir.

"Okay." I sidestepped him, not even sure why I was angry that he would joke about hooking up with some girl I didn't even know. It really wasn't all that funny to my little virgin ears. If anything, it made me want to smack him.

"What'd I do?" He stepped in front of me and grasped my arms. His eyes scanned me from head to toe as his hands caressed upward toward my shoulders. His smile was mocking. And suddenly I wanted to be anywhere but in the hall with this very attractive boy who was used to getting exactly what he wanted regardless of the consequences.

I opened my mouth to speak, but stopped when I felt a warm hand grip my shoulder.

"Really, Demetri? Begging isn't your style." It had to be Alec.

Demetri's face immediately broke into a grin. "I'm sorry, Nat. He's right. I don't beg. I don't usually have to, but you make me want to."

I was officially pinned between two of the hottest guys on the planet and all I could think about was not passing out. Demetri was in front of me, all 6'4" and packed muscle. I staggered backward only to find myself up against the same thing. Only Alec smelled like expensive cologne. The type that should burn your nostrils but instead makes you want to close your eyes and moan.

It was probably Abercrombie. I swear they put pheromones in that stuff.

"Run along," Alec said over the top of my head.

Demetri nodded once and walked away, but not before giving me a seductive wink.

I exhaled, not realizing I had been holding my breath. Alec's hand moved across my shoulder until his arm was around me. I stumbled in shock.

"You sure do that a lot," he said without looking at me.

I watched his face as his eyes scanned the hallways. He was walking me out the door as if it was the most natural thing in the world. Clearly he had lost his mind.

"Trip?" I offered.

He nodded.

Apparently Demetri got the personality in this family.

"I can't help it, I'm clumsy." I shrugged, liking the way the weight of his arm felt on my neck and shoulders.

"Yes. You are."

"Well…" I stepped out of his embrace. "As stimulating as this conversation's been I got a ton of homework tonight, so I'll see ya later." I walked away but froze in my tracks when I heard gut-wrenching laughter behind me.

I whipped around and truly wished I would have just kept walking. Then I wouldn't have seen the way Alec's smile totally transformed his face. The twinkling green eyes basically glowing on the tan skin. He lifted his hands into the air in surrender and approached me.

My inability to breath was not helping the situation.

"You think I'm boring, don't you?"Alec seemed amused as he leaned in closer to me.

Exhausted, I laughed and put my hands on my hips, fighting to keep myself from making eye contact. "Yes. But you're pretty to look at, so as long as someone doesn't scratch your face off, you'll always have that!"

I slugged him like we were on some sort of baseball team and laughed. The look of horror on his face was priceless. Clearly, he was also used to getting exactly what he wanted.

"Sorry." Still laughing he shoved his hands in his pockets. "I'm not used to much social interaction."

"Says the poor afflicted rock star."

"Girl's got bite, I like that." He winked. "Can I walk you to your car?"

"Are we stuck in the fifties?"

"It is Seaside," he countered, offering me his arm.

Well, really what else could I do but take him up on the offer? I rolled my eyes and took it. "You gonna carry my books too?"

"Wait, do guys still do that?"

"It is Seaside," I reminded him.

He took my books as if they weighed about a pound and walked me to my truck.

Alec's eyes scanned the ride in approval. "Beautiful girl, drives a truck, hates rock stars... Hmm, I just might write a song about you."

My heart hammered in my chest but I kept myself in check. "Is this where I'm supposed to swoon and tattoo your name on my ass?"

"You don't have to swoon." He leaned in, his body shielding me from the school and all air that smelled like anything other than his cologne. "But can you make sure to spell it with just one L?"

I rolled my eyes. "Why are you here?"

"I like you."

"Thanks," I muttered, feeling that all too familiar blush. "But I meant Seaside, Oregon. It's literally the most boring place on Earth. Well, I guess that's not true. That title actually goes to Boring, Oregon."

His smile tightened a bit as he licked his lips and then looked away. "I'll see you later, Nat."

He walked off without an explanation. His mood had changed again.

I jumped into my car and shook my head. This had to have been the weirdest day in my existence.

My cell rang. I slipped it out of my pocket. "Crap!" It wasn't mine. I still had Alec's cell. How could I have forgotten that?

I looked at the screen. It was flashing my number. I

wanted to drop the cell like a hot potato or at least hide it or something. Oh my gosh, he's going to think I seriously stole his cell phone like some crazy stalker!

Without any other option, I answered with a shaky hello.

"Naughty girl stole my brother's cell phone," the voice said mockingly.

"Hey, Demetri."

"Hey yourself." His voice sounded deeper on the phone. My body shivered involuntarily.

After a few awkward seconds I asked, "Is there something you needed?"

"That depends."

"On?"

"If you're offering to help me with my… needs."

"You're disgusting."

"Aw, thanks sweetheart."

"Look." My hands shook as I tried to calm myself down. "I didn't mean to keep Alec's phone. Is there a place I can drop it off or something?"

Silence and then, "Why don't you just keep it until tomorrow? We'll see you at school and I'll make the swap."

"He's going to know his phone's missing. Besides, he has mine."

"I know. I've already hacked into it. High School Musical, Nat, really?"

I groaned aloud and fought the urge to bang my head against the steering wheel. "It's good running music."

"So is the entire Hannah Montana soundtrack. Doesn't mean you put it on your playlist, Nat."

"Wait. How do you know the Hannah Montana soundtrack is good running music?"

"That's beside the point. We're talking about you now."

"Did you need anything else?" I snapped.

"Are you offering?"

"Bye, Demetri." I hit end and ignored the silly butterflies

that had taken up permanent residence in my stomach. I refused to be one of those girls.

I looked back at the school. It was as if you could see a wave of lust blow through the front door as girls walked out and began texting on their phones, hiking up their skirts, and giggling obnoxiously. No doubt each of them wanted a chance with the guys. And again, I refused to be one of those girls. If anything, it made me want to put on baggy sweats just so I could set myself apart from the groupies.

At any rate, I had a crap-load of homework but my job was calling my name. I quickly put the truck in drive and made my way over to Seaside Taffy.

Chapter Three

"Hey Evan," I called. The door jingled when I walked in. I was immediately hit with the sweet smell of taffy and homemade ice cream cones.

"Nat, didn't think you'd make it." Evan gave me a wicked grin and nodded his head in approval. "Had a little bad boy run-in in the school parking lot, did ya?"

"I hate you."

I threw on my pink Seaside Taffy visor and tied my apron.

"You want him."

"Who?" I grabbed a piece of taffy and popped it in my mouth.

Evan punched me in the shoulder like I was a dude and laughed. "Who cares!? All the girls want them both. I would give my right n—"

"Language." Our boss suddenly appeared from the back office and narrowed his eyes at us.

Evan lifted up his hands in surrender. "I was going to say..." Evan bit his lip in thought.

I rolled my eyes. "Sorry, Mr. Dexter. I'll be sure to keep

Evan on a short leash today."

Mr. Dexter was really weird about any of his employees using slang or bad language. In fact, he preferred we say golly instead of gosh. True story. Maybe it was because the entire store looked like the fifties threw up on it. At any rate, poor Evan still hadn't received a raise, even after working there for a year. He kept getting yellow slips in his employee box to remind him not to say things like ass to children.

Mr. Dexter disappeared and shut the office door behind him.

I started cutting the taffy to give out for free samples.

"So…" Evan came up beside me. "You going to tell me what Mr. Rock Star wanted?"

I shrugged. "He was just taking my books to my car."

Evan choked on a piece of taffy. "Nat, I promise you, he wanted to take more than your books to your car."

"That doesn't even make sense."

"Yes it does," Evan argued. "He wanted to take you to your car and throw you in the backseat, have his way with you, have sweaty, angry, se—"

"Evan?" Mr. Dexter appeared behind us again.

I bit my tongue to keep from laughing.

Evan sighed. "I was going to say sweaty, angry…"

The guy really needed to think on the spot better.

With a curse, Evan followed Mr. Dexter into the back room, most likely to get another yellow slip, and I continued cutting the taffy. Today was a shorter shift, which I was thankful for. My concentration wasn't exactly on.

Alec's phone buzzed in my pocket.

I looked back at the office door to make sure it was closed, then pulled it out.

I FND IT OFFNSV THT U PSWD PRTCTD UR FB.

I laughed and texted him back.

I FND IT OFFNSV THT UR TRYNG 2 HAK MY FB. DO U HV NO 1 ELS 2 TORTURE?

I slipped the phone back into my jeans pocket and sighed.

Within seconds he texted me back. Okay, so I was grinning like an idiot. I couldn't help it.

NO. NO. I DNT. BESIDES. I CHOOSE U. U R MY VICTIM. & I WILL HAK UR FB & TWTR IF ITS THE LST THNG I DO. SIGH. IM BORD. THS IS WHT MY LFE HS COME 2.

I texted him back quickly. *I RFSE 2 FEEL SRY 4 U. UR A RKSTR. GT OVR IT. Y DNT U WRT A SONG? HA HA.*

The office door swung open. I nearly dropped the phone, but managed to slip it into my pocket just as Evan came out.

"I'm never getting a raise."

I raised an eyebrow. "Did you really think you would? You do have this problem where all you do is talk and talk and talk and—"

"I get it, Nat." He cut me off and turned on the radio.

The announcer was gushing about AD2. "*...and the guys are rumored to be going to school at Seaside! Here's their latest hit, 'Without'.*"

"I have a feeling I'm going to want to burn every AD2 poster I see before the year's out," I said.

"Ouch."

I looked up. Alec Daniels was standing right in front of me. Ripped jeans, ripped arms, and brooding stare. I gulped.

"Want some taffy?"

I want to die. I just offered Alec Daniels taffy like he was a five-year-old in need of a sugar rush.

"Uh, sure." He grabbed a freshly cut piece and tossed it into his mouth. I couldn't help but watch as he licked his lips. Gosh, I needed to get out more or at least date. I was turning into every other girl.

Evan nudged me in the side.

"Ugh." *Great, Nat. Brilliant start*. "Can I help you with something?"

Alec leaned forward, his hands clenching the counter top.

"Yup. I just need a bag of taffy. It's for my brother."

"Okay, what kind?"

Alec looked around, his eyes widened as he took in the hundreds of flavors. "Um, I…"

I laughed. "Here let me help." I walked around the counter and grabbed a bag. "Everything's labeled on the side. Here's fruit flavors, and this aisle has the more odd flavors like buttered popcorn, and down here is the alcohol-flavored ones."

"That aisle." He pointed to the alcohol one. "That's perfect."

I wasn't about to butt in and ask why, so I went to the aisle and picked a few from every bin. "Here you go."

His hand brushed mine as he grabbed the bag. I felt myself blush. I took a step back and quickly returned to the counter.

I could feel his stare on me as he followed me back.

"How much?"

I took the bag and weighed it. "Fifteen dollars and ninety-two cents."

Alec reached back into his jeans and pulled out his wallet. He placed a fifty on the counter. "Keep the change. Thanks, Nat." He glanced toward Evan and nodded.

It was silent for about five minutes after Alec left.

"And again…" Evan laughed next to me. "I'd give my right nut to—"

"Evan!" Mr. Dexter yelled.

I patted Evan on the back and tried to be nonchalant. But there was something about Alec that drew me toward him. He seemed so different than Demetri, so guarded. I pulled out the phone and then wanted to smack myself. I could have given Alec his phone back. He must think I wanted to hold it hostage or something. And what type of person doesn't password protect their own phone? Especially a celebrity.

I looked at the phone again and hit pictures.

He had over three hundred.

I knew it was wrong to scroll through them. Just as my finger touched the first one, Mr. Dexter's voice rang loud and clear through the store. I quickly put the phone away and finished my shift.

Chapter Four

I desperately needed to give that cursed phone back to Alec and Demetri. I seriously had to set it away from my homework station, so I wouldn't be tempted to peek at the pictures. It didn't help that Demetri felt the need to text me every second annoying the heck out of me and making me smile more than I'd care to admit.

The phone buzzed again.

STP IGNRNG ME. LTS GO PRTY.

I rolled my eyes and quickly texted back. *I DNT PRTY. I'M UNDRAGE. SO R U. DNT U HV HMWK?*

The same math problem I'd been working on for the past hour stared back at me. The phone buzzed again.

I SUK AT MTH. I ND HLP. I MAY GT A TUTOR...U UP 4 THE JB?

I bit my lip. *U DO KNW A TUTOR ISNT A PROSTITUTE, RT?*

His reply was quick. *DAMN, I KNEW I HD THSE 2 MXD UP.*

I laughed and tucked the sleek phone under my pillow in bed. I needed to think about getting to sleep if I was going to face those two guys tomorrow without fainting at their feet. I yawned and closed my math book, then turned off my bedroom's lights and climbed into bed. On impulse I pulled out Alec's phone and texted Demetri goodnight. He didn't reply. I shouldn't have been upset over it. But I kind of was. I told myself to stop being stupid as I waited for the screen to blink with his message. I closed my eyes and then five minutes later.

I checked the phone again. No messages.

My thumb hovered over the pictures.

With a curse, I clicked on the icon and scrolled through them.

Immediately, I wished I wouldn't have.

The pictures were amazing. Not your typical rock star bad boy pictures. But pictures of sunsets, vacations, and… puppies? Oh my gosh! No way was this for real. Alec was supposed to have pictures of strippers and whores. It just showed how little I really knew about him. I suspected he was the bad boy of the bunch, but then again, Demetri was always shown as being the player between the two of them, at least on the gossip sites and entertainment TV.

I hated that I was curious about Alec. It made me uncomfortable to know that he was so closed off. It was like crack to me. I wanted to be the girl to figure out his secrets. And I knew that never ended well for anyone.

With a yawn I placed the phone on the nightstand and went to sleep.

****

I felt dead on my feet as I opened my locker the next day at school. I hadn't seen either of the guys, but I knew they had to be somewhere if the shrieks echoing through the hallways were any indication.

I sighed and shoved my math book in the place of my

history book.

"Nat." Demetri breathed down my neck.

I swore and turned around. "You scared the crap out of me!"

He grinned unapologetically and held out my pathetic phone. "I made a few changes to your settings and stuff. Hope you don't mind."

I looked down to see my screensaver a picture of Demetri's naked chest. Awesome. I felt a hot blush wash over my cheeks.

"Thanks." I grabbed the phone and shoved Alec's into his hand.

He didn't move.

I waited.

He looked at me like I was a puzzle. "Wanna walk to class?"

If he kept looking at me like that I was going to pass out and he'd have to carry me to class, only to have me pass out again because he was carrying me. "Um, sure." I grabbed my books and walked with him.

The class was only a few feet away, but it felt like miles. People whispered behind their books as we passed, and then Demetri put his hand on my lower back.

I nearly jumped out of my skin.

"Chill." He chuckled as we made it into the classroom.

All eyes darted to us.

All except Alec's.

I gulped and took a seat. Once the teacher began taking roll I stole a glance at him. Alec was staring at me. He wasn't smiling. In fact he looked irritated, either that or angry. I wasn't sure. I offered him an apologetic smile. He ignored me and turned back to the teacher.

****

By the end of their first week, the other kids were beginning to return to normal. Girls stopped fainting in the hallways and the guys weren't signing near as many autographs. Demetri walked me to class every day and Alec found great pleasure in brooding all the time. It made me uncomfortable how much he backed off once Demetri and I started talking more. If I was being completely honest, a part of me was a bit upset that he and I couldn't have the same relationship Demetri and I did. But then again, who was I to be upset about anything? I mean he was everything. I was nothing.

I was so lost in my thoughts that I didn't hear anyone approach.

Someone tapped me on the shoulder. I dropped all my books to the floor.

"Geez, Nat, you're so jumpy." Demetri knelt down to pick up all my books and then dumped them in my locker. "I need help."

My eyes narrowed. "With?" I always had to be direct with Demetri. He was the type of guy who could get even the most moral of girls into bed.

"Math. Remember? I suck?"

"You're asking me for help?"

He shrugged. "We're friends."

Oh. I suddenly felt kinda guilty. I was officially going to delete all the gossip sites from my computer. The guy couldn't be as bad the media made him out to be, and he'd been really nice the past week. At least when he wasn't trying to get me to go to parties or flirt back with him.

"Well…" I studied him for a minute. He didn't seem to have any ulterior motive. In fact his eyes shone with desperation. "I guess I can help you, I have to finish all my stuff first. Do you mean tonight?"

"I mean tonight." He chuckled. "How about I come over around eight, would that be okay?"

"Yeah, um… sure." I choked on my words.

"Cool. Thanks, Nat!"

He hit me in the arm and ran down the hall, leaving me to wonder what the heck just happened. Crap, I was under his spell just like everyone else.

I banged my head against the locker. Maybe it would jostle my memory, remind me why I shouldn't get close to a guy whose idea of prioritizing included picking which girls he would sleep with before leaving Seaside and putting them in a chronological list."Headache?" A smooth voice said from behind me.

Maybe it was all a game? AD2 thought it would be fun to torture the local girl and make her life confusing and hormonal.

"Alec." I breathed.

He licked his lips and then looked down at the floor. "Do you have any more taffy?"

"Huh?" Not what I was expecting.

"You mean now?"

He nodded.

Was he for real? "Um, I have a few pieces in my bag, why?"

His shoulders sagged in relief.

Without waiting for him to answer, I pulled out a few pieces and handed them over. He popped all three in his mouth and moaned. I felt the rumble of his moan all the way down to my toes.

"Thank God."

"So brooding Rock Star has a thing for taffy?"

Alec grinned the first grin I'd seen since his first day at school. "You could say that. Or maybe Rock Star just needs something in his mouth ever since he quit smoking."

"And the world makes sense again." I nodded. "Ever try lollipops?"

"Yup." He cursed. "Too much sugar."

"Gum?" I offered.

Somehow we had gotten from my locker to the front doors.

"Loses flavor."

I nodded again. "So taffy is your best bet."

He grinned again. He was beautiful. Even more beautiful than Demetri when he smiled. Crap! I needed to help him with his homework and I still had to work and finish mine! "I gotta go, Alec!"

His eyes narrowed. He looked unsure, and then he nodded and walked off in the other direction without even saying goodbye.

By the time my work shift was over, I only had a half hour to do homework before Demetri came over for help.

Wait.

He didn't even ask for directions and he just invited himself to my house. Wasn't that a bit strange? I knew he had my number saved so maybe he was going to text me for directions later?

I leaned against the truck. I seriously had no more energy left after today. Maybe I liked boring better than interesting. I still couldn't figure out why these two guys were even giving me attention.

I shrugged and walked into the house.

Chapter Five

I had officially turned into "that girl". The one who watches the clock as the hand goes around and around. It was eight, and he still wasn't here. He was going to be late. By one minute. And I, being the boring, paranoid, oh so socially-sheltered girl that I was, allowed myself to sweat over that simple fact.

Maybe he found another girl to help him?

Or guy, it didn't always have to be about girls.

I tore my gaze from the clock and went to the fridge to grab a soda. If he wasn't coming it was fine. I would be fine. It's not like I didn't have stuff to do.

Like watch Wheel of Fortune, or scream at The Bachelor. How depressing.

I looked at the clock again.

One minute? It had only been one minute?

I banged my head against the counter loud enough to make a noise.

"Rough night, beautiful?" The voice crooned from across the hall.

My head jerked up to see Demetri walking toward me

from my mom's office. What the—?

"What are you doing here?"

My mom walked out of the office, Alec followed her.

It was like all my nightmares come true.

"Oh, hi, Honey!" Mom adjusted her glasses and walked to the fridge to grab a bottle of water. "My next client should be here in about ten, so I'll be up late tonight. Have fun studying!"

She walked back into her office and shut the door.

"Explain. Now." I directed my voice toward both of them, since they were both guilty, and looking anywhere but at my face.

Alec was the first to open his mouth. "I have…" He looked down at his feet and cursed.

Demetri laughed. "He has a little problem." He offered Alec a shrug and walked over to where I sat. "It's why we're here."

"Aren't their psychiatrists in L.A.? Canada? I mean, why my mom? Why here?"

Alec mumbled something under his breath and walked out of the house slamming the door behind him.

"Sorry." Demetri put his arm around my shoulder in a side hug then released me. "It's kind of a secret, though I don't think it's going to stay that way for long."

I clenched my teeth and backed away. "Mind filling me in?"

"If you are the math genius I'm hoping you are then yes, I promise I'll fill you in. After homework."

"That sounds an awful lot like bribery." I glared.

Demetri shrugged. "It is. Hey you got any food? I'm starving!"

It was like having Evan in the house. If Evan happened to be so good looking it hurt your eyes to stare at him, and had a body of a god. Yeah, it was practically the same thing.

I walked to the fridge and searched out the leftover pot

roast. "This is pot roast. Those," I pointed, "Are potatoes, and these are carrots." I grabbed his hand and led him to the plates. "This is a plate."

He glared.

"You put the food on the plate, and then you come over here." I opened the microwave and put the food inside. "Think you can handle it from here, Rock Star?"

His glare should have frightened me. Instead it made me even angrier than before. Both of the boys just barged into my life without any explanation, and now they're seeing my mom? Neither of them will answer any questions, and Demetri thinks he's some sort of god!

He shut the microwave and pressed all the right buttons. "I'm trying to decide if I like you or if you irritate me."

I shrugged like it didn't matter and walked to the counter.

He ate in silence, like he really was starving. But that was silly. He was a rock star. Didn't they pay people to cook for them?

"Thanks," he said, picking up his plate and cleaning it before placing it into the dishwasher. He picked up my empty plate and did the same thing, then made a grand gesture of washing off the counters.

Pretty sure I wanted to get hit by a truck for my mean attitude.

"Sorry."

"I swear." He threw the dishrag down. "It's always the same!" He roughly tugged the chair out and sat down in it. "Either girls want to screw my brains out, or they think I'm a freaking idiot! Like I don't know how to get my own food or iron my own clothes. As if everything's been easy for me. No struggles, nothing. Just a golden boy with a damn golden guitar."

His mental break down made me feel like the worst type of person in the world. I kind of wanted to cry.

"I-I'm sorry." I put my hand on his and exhaled. "I didn't mean to assume anything."

His brow furrowed. "Are you actually apologizing, Miss High and Mighty?"

"Yes?"

"Good." He grinned. "Because I was totally kidding. I love my life and I deserve to be kicked in the balls right about now for making you almost cry."

I lunged for him.

I blamed the soda I had chugged minutes before his arrival.

His shocked expression turned into laughter as I pushed him to the ground and began using all my MMA class moves on his sorry ass.

His arm was locked before he even knew what was going on.

Feeling kinda cocky, I shot him a smug smile.

"That's how it's gonna be, huh?" His muscles flexed.

I nodded.

"Fine."

"Fine." I squeezed, making the arm bar tighter.

He chuckled, and maneuvered himself out of the hold faster than I'd seen anyone in my life, including Evan who regularly took classes at the local gym.

In seconds he was straddling me, looking quite pleased with himself.

"Not that I didn't deserve to get my ass kicked," he said out of breath. "But, I kind of like this position better."

I squirmed beneath him.

"And better… and better."

I yelled. It didn't help. If anything it made him laugh harder until exhaustion set in and I joined him.

He leaned down and kissed the top of my forehead. "Math?"

"As long you refrain from making me cry or wanting to

punch you, then yes, we can do math." I sighed, a little breathless from the fact that the rock god had just kissed my forehead.

He seemed to think about it for a minute then nodded his head.

Minutes after starting math I realized two things. One, he was dead serious about needing help, and two, he was actually serious about wanting to get things right.

While he was working on the last problem I stole a glance at the clock, it was already ten.

"You live here your whole life?" he asked not looking up from the paper.

"Uh, yeah." I nervously started tapping my pencil. "You always live in Canada?"

Dumb question, everyone knew they resided in L.A. now, but I wanted to hear it from him.

"Five houses." He erased his problem and squinted. "One in British Columbia, a beach house in Malibu, a penthouse in New York, a flat in London, and finally a cottage in good ol' Seaside."

I'm sure my mouth was open in shock. That's more houses than me and my friends put together.

Once I was able to get my thoughts back on track I asked, "Why Seaside?"

"And that, I do not have to answer until after homework. You promised."

"Fine." I sighed then grabbed the paper. He folded his hands behind his head and leaned back in the chair.

His work took him a long time, and I could see why. His hand writing was meticulous, every word formed perfectly. He wrote how he talked. It was impressive, to say the least. Usually it was impossible to read guys' handwriting. The work was perfect except for one.

"This one." I pointed it out. "You used the wrong formula."

"I know." He shrugged.

"Not following, Demetri." I smacked his arm with my pencil.

"I'm just tired of being perfect, so I figured I would create a small flaw in my homework. Adds character I hear."

I nodded my head. "And you're officially impossible. All right, if you want imperfection who am I to disagree?"

"Come on!" He jolted from his chair and grabbed my hand before I could say anything except a slur of "Huh?" The guy was bipolar! How did we go from discussing math to running to my door like there was a fire?

I nearly tripped over my North Face as I pulled it off the coat rack. I was beginning to suspect that the guys were on drugs. Why else would they be so all over the place? Almost erratic in their behavior?

"Come on." He nodded to the North Face in my hand. "Put it on. It's kinda chilly."

I bit my lip in frustration, but did it anyways because it really was starting to get cold and windy. "Where are we going?"

"To the beach. To talk." And that was the only explanation I got as he led me down our dock onto the large white sand beach.

Seaside would be the perfect vacation spot if the weather could decide what it wanted to be. One day it could be a hundred degrees outside, the next day you could see your breath. That was The Pacific Coast for you, though. The beaches were amazing, but you were lucky if you had a few sunny days in a row. That didn't hinder tourism; it just meant that during the fall months, like October, there weren't nearly as many people around.

The beach was abandoned. It was eerily quiet. The only sound came from the waves as they rolled across the sand. Demetri held my hand in his as we ventured closer to the waves.

"Wanna skinny dip?"

"Yes," I answered enthusiastically. "I would love to die at eighteen. Do you have any idea how cold that water is?"

"I don't remember it being that bad." He shrugged and threw off his shoes and socks, with not so much as a glance in my direction he ran into the water.

Curses exploded into the stillness of the night.

I laughed as he came running back.

"Told ya." I held out his socks and shoes.

"Remind me to listen to you from here on out, on everything." He shuddered and took his stuff but threw it on the beach and sat.

"Join me?" He patted the sand next to him. Something about his impulsiveness called to me. Demetri seemed to have no plan, no agenda. It was all about being in the moment. I kind of envied him, even if he was a little into himself. But I guess I would be too if I had people stripping in front of me and telling me I was some sort of rock god.

"So, Seaside." I played with the sand in front of me.

"Seaside." He drew his knees up and leaned his head against them. "It's not really my story to tell."

"Oh, so there's a whole story?"

Demetri laughed. I could see the outline of his mouth, because his teeth were so white. "Yeah, you could say that. Or really there are two stories. The first story is the cover, the second is the truth."

"Which one do I get?"

"I'm still deciding." The laughter left his face as his eyes met mine. Those clear blue eyes focused on my lips as he leaned closer.

I was frozen in place. I couldn't pull away even if I wanted to. And the closer he came to touching my lips, the more I wanted his kiss.

My tongue slipped out to wet my lips as he closed the final distance between us. The minute his mouth met mine, I gasped.

His mouth was so different than the air around us. Where everything was cold, he was hot, so warm and inviting. His hands reached to cup my face as his tongue slipped beyond the barrier of my lips. He didn't attack me, nor did he aggressively push me down. I was almost disappointed when he pulled back.

Demetri's eyes were hooded; he leaned back in and kissed my lips briefly before again pulling back and cursing. "Sorry."

Sorry? He's sorry? He just gave me the best kiss of my life, my first kiss, and he's sorry.

Embarrassed, I quickly got to my feet and brushed off the sand.

"Wait." His hand jetted out and grabbed mine. "I didn't mean I'm sorry about the kiss. I've never been less sorry in my life about a kiss. I'm just sorry I used it as a way to get you to stop asking about why we're here."

"Okay," I said trying to wrap my mind around his explanation. Our hands were still intertwined. The memory of his lips burned across mine. I fought to keep my attitude indifferent when all I wanted to do was jump on top of him and beg him to kiss me again.

He rose from his seat and sighed. "We're on a break from touring and making music. We've been told quite plainly that we need to back off for a while, let things calm down in our personal lives before we ruin our careers."

"Okay," I said, mentally going through all the stuff I had read on the news for the past few weeks. None of it even hinted towards them pulling a stunt like this. And then it hit me. "That's what's going to be on the news tomorrow, huh?"

He nodded.

"So you told me the lie."

He paused, then nodded again.

I guess I hadn't given him a reason to trust me. It still

stung that he didn't. Then again, he didn't know me at all. If anything, I could be the type of girl that would gossip about our private conversations, even our kiss.

I wasn't that girl.

I immediately felt the need to tell him, but he didn't give me a chance. He dropped back down on the sand and jerked me down so hard I fell on top of him. He flipped me onto my back and opened his mouth to mine.

He tasted so good. His hands pinned mine to the sand as his tongue explored my mouth and he bit at my lower lip.

I moaned when he turned away and cursed. Are you trying to distract me?"

"Does it matter?" he asked out of breath.

I nodded.

His eyes got sad. "Then yeah, I am."

"Get off me." I tried to push him away, but he wouldn't budge. "I said get off!"

I wasn't used to people not listening to me. This boy was more confusing than any I had ever come across... well, except Alec. He took the cake on that one.

"I like you," was all he said. As if that explained why he would take advantage of me by kissing me.

"Well, I don't like you."

He laughed and nibbled on my ear. "Yeah, actually, I think you do."

Irritated, I pushed his chest again, but his lips moved to my neck as he sucked near my collarbone, his tongue twirled in circles as his teeth lightly bit down.

I pulled him closer to me. I didn't want any space between our bodies. I wasn't even cold any more. No, I was on fire. I wanted him more than anything in the world.

"We have school in the morning," he whispered in my ear. Crap even school sounded sexy on his lips.

I groaned. "I know."

"We should go." But he didn't move.

"Yep." I really had no excuse for my behavior as I clenched him tighter and covered my mouth with his.

He chuckled beneath my kiss, then lifted me over his body so I was straddling him. I kissed down his neck, like he had mine. He groaned and then cursed pulling my hands back. "If you keep doing that, this night is going to end very very well, and it can't." He cursed again and covered his eyes with his hand. "And if you keep looking at me like you want to eat me, I'm most likely going to strip you naked and have my way with you."

No boy had ever talked to me like that before. I wasn't sure if I was supposed to be offended or complimented. Struggling with my answer, I stayed silent, my brows furrowed.

Chuckling, he reached up and kissed my mouth softly. "Let me put this in a way you'll understand. I want you more than I should after only knowing you a day. And I'm used to getting what I want. If you stay, I'll get it. And you don't deserve that."

I jerked away and nodded my head as I got to my feet.

"I need a minute," he shook his head and then closed his eyes as he lay in the sand. It looked like he was meditating.

My body was still on fire and trembling from our interaction.

After a few silent minutes, he dusted off the sand and grabbed my hand. "Do you really want to know why we're here?"

I clenched his hand tightly. "Yes!"

"Good." He smirked and pulled me into a side hug, kissing my head. "Maybe if you keep hanging out with me, I'll tell you."

I jerked away and swatted him.

We stopped in front of my house. I looked around for a car but saw nothing.

"Need a ride?" I called after him as he disappeared

further down the road.

"Didn't think you were that kind girl." He called back winking as he quickly turned and walked into the house right next to mine.

Holy crap. The brothers were living next door to me. Could it get any worse?

"I meant in a car!" I yelled back upset.

"Ooh!" He lifted his hands in the air. "Even better!"

"I hate you!"

"No, you don't!" He laughed before walking into the large house next door.

One thing I knew for sure. It was going to be a long school year.

Chapter Six

I woke up Friday ready to face the day. Well, sort of. I hadn't run the day before. I knew if I wanted to actually make it through track season this spring that I needed to keep training. Besides, I had to be up extra early for that stupid Homecoming meeting. Especially considering I had missed two in a row and was now on Alesha's crap list. Why had I agreed to serving on the committee in the first place? Oh right, because my friend forced me into it and Evan claimed he needed someone who wasn't currently trying to get into his pants. Which was totally how he and Alesha acted around each other. She'd flutter her eyelashes, he'd roll his eyes, and seconds later they'd be making out in the closet. Evan always claimed temporary insanity. However, I knew the truth. He wanted her just as bad. They just didn't know how to jump out of the friends with benefits zone. But what guy would want that especially if Alesha was already giving him all the benefits?

I threw the covers back, sleepily rolled out of bed, and put on my workout gear. I twisted my hair into a ponytail and ran down the stairs out the front door.

The air was crisp and frigid. It was one of the colder mornings, but at least the wind wasn't blowing as hard as it normally was. I don't know why but running in the wind totally put me in a foul mood.

I stretched and quickly put on my gloves so my fingers wouldn't freeze.

"Didn't take you for the type that exercised," a voice said to my right.

I turned and came face to face with Alec. He was wearing workout gear and a baseball cap. He almost looked… normal. Well, as normal as a gorgeous guy could look.

I shook my head. "Yeah well, I didn't take you for the type to do anything but sit and brood, so I guess we're even, huh?"

Laughing, he removed his hat and rubbed his hair down before putting it back on again. "Want some company?"

Out of all the things he could have said, that was the last I expected. "You want to run with me?"

"I think I can keep up."

"I run fast."

"Okay," he seemed unaffected.

"I listen to music."

He held up his iPhone. The same one I had shamelessly stalked not a few days ago.

Gulping, I nodded my head. "Sounds great." But it wasn't great. For some reason Alec made me more uncomfortable than Demetri. At least with Demetri I knew what to expect. He'd flirt, kiss you senseless, shower you with compliments, and you'd hold your breath praying he wouldn't cheat on you.

Alec was… well, he was Alec. There was something mysterious about him. At least running would make it so we didn't talk too much. I was still curious about why they were here in the first place, but if I couldn't get it out of Demetri the night before, than I sure wasn't going to get his brother to budge in that area.

"Ready?" I watched as he turned on his music and put his headphones in. With a quick nod in my direction he was off.

We ran a mile in silence.

I never looked in his direction. But it was hard to keep my eyes focused on the road when I was running with some mysterious yet famous bad boy.

Once we reached the second mile I was ready to yell. He was staring at me. I could feel his gaze. I was practically burning up from head to toe with mortification. Finally I stopped in my tracks and found the ear buds that had been tucked in my pocket. I needed to listen to music if I was going to have to put up with his brooding stare.

I slid ear buds into my ears but didn't turn on the music. "What!"

Alec bit his lip and reached up to pull out his ear buds. "I'm just surprised."

"Do I even want to know?" I stretched my arms.

He moved behind me and gently tugged them into a tighter stretch then whispered in my ear, "You tripped over your own feet twice yesterday. I wasn't sure you could even walk in a straight line until now."

"I'm in track."

His warm chuckle gave me shivers as he moved my arms behind my back and crossed them so that my shoulders and chest were getting a better stretch.

"That explains the body."

"What?" I jerked away from him and turned around.

"Your body." He looked me up from head to toe then met my gaze. "You have long legs."

The way he said it, almost in reverence. Confused, I squinted at him. Normally, guys said things like *you're hot*, or *nice bod*. Instead, he just complimented the length of my legs like I was some sort of giant. I wasn't sure why I felt a blush coming on. Maybe it was because his compliment didn't make me feel objectified, but more special. I seriously needed to get out more.

"What?" Alec grinned. I hated it when he smiled at me like that. As if I was his sun, moon, and stars. When clearly, that was not the case.

"You can't just walk around saying things like that to girls."

"Just did." He shrugged. "But I guess in a way you're right. I shouldn't say things like that to my brother's girl. There's rules for that and all."

Irritated, I glared at him and grabbed my phone to change songs. "I'm not his girl."

Alec whistled. "Don't tell him that. Plus, I saw the two of you last night."

"Studying?" Why was I so hopeful that he didn't see us later that night?

"At the beach," Alec confirmed, his eyes narrowing before he broke out into another earth-shattering grin. "But it's cool. Demetri likes you. Look." Alec sat on the edge of the fence near the boardwalk. "I want to be your friend. I'm not going to lie and say I'm not angry that my brother got to you first. But I'll overlook your obvious lack of good judgment if you promise you'll come to me if you need anything. Okay?"

I nodded slowly, my heart thumping way too loud for us to be in the friend zone or any zone near it.

"Cool." He grabbed my phone. "Justin Bieber, Nat? Really?"

I felt myself flush. "It's good running music!"

"I'm a little hurt. Are we even on here?" My worst nightmares were coming true as he scrolled through the playlist.

"Give me that!" I lunged for him. Unlike his brother, he wasn't okay with allowing a girl to win. He held me off with one arm. I kicked. He only laughed harder.

"No way! You love me!" He jumped up and down and waved his hands in the air. This was not the Alec I knew. The Alec I knew brooded. What the heck?

"Give that back." Teeth clenched I held out my hand.

"Are you blushing?" he teased.

"No, I'm just, winded." Lame answer, Nat. Lame answer!

"I like this playlist best too."

I cursed and looked down at my phone, when he handed it back to me it was on the playlist marked. Crush.

I wanted to kill him.

"Want me to sing to you right now?" he asked, amusement making his eyes twinkle more than usual.

"No, I kind of want to jump into the ocean and drown myself though."

"I'm not worth it, and neither is Justin Bieber. Don't let me see that crap on your run mix again." He put his ear buds in.

I reached for his phone, but he had it in his pocket before I could snatch it. "What do you listen to?"

"Myself, of course." He laughed as he set the pace for our run back.

"Doubt it."

"Wanna bet?" He stopped.

"Yup." I knew the guy probably had himself on his playlist it only made sense, but I highly doubted he actually listened to himself sing, that would be vain, and he didn't seem the type. Now, Demetri on the other hand…

"Fine. I win, you have to go to Evan's party with me next Friday. You win, I'll let you drive my car for a week."

"What kind of car?" I asked. I was skeptical since I hadn't since either of their rides over the past week. Then again, I hadn't exactly stalked them like the rest of the student body.

"What kind of car do you think I drive?"

I liked this side of Alec, the playful one. He reminded me of Demetri only more devastating. I'm sure any girl on the opposite end of that smile would willingly throw their V card, no questions asked. "I'm guessing you drive something classy, dark. Hmm, black Mercedes, tinted windows?" As I watched the sweat trickle down his cheek, I could almost pretend like he was a normal person… almost. My comfort level with Alec had definitely changed.

"Not even close, but it's nice. I promise."

"Fine." I held out my hand. "Hand it over."

He placed the phone in my hands. I gasped. He really was listening to himself, but it didn't say AD2 it said *Alec Daniels*.

"What's this?"

He shrugged.

I unplugged his ear phones and slipped mine in.

The music wasn't the usual techno that the guys were famous for. It was… raw. It made me want to cry. My heart lurched when his voice reached the high notes. It was an acoustic track, and then the music stopped and he was talking about changing the verse. The music started again and his voice reached the same painful heights that made me tremble.

Shaking, I handed the phone back. "Is that going on your next album?"

"Nope." He laughed bitterly. "That will never see the light of day. Not if my brother has anything to do with it."

"Why?" I blurted.

He shrugged. Should have known he wouldn't give me any details. "So this party…" He placed his phone back in his pocket. "I'll pick you up at seven."

I rolled my eyes. "A bet's a bet."

"Yes it is." Alec said, starting to run again. I followed him. We ended the run in silence. He waved as he ran inside. I might be late for my school meeting, but it was all worth it.

Mom had yet again fallen asleep in her office.

I yelled goodbye.

Silence greeted me.

I hated being ignored so much, but the only other option would be to charge into her room and share my feelings. I'd rather be ignored than be a client.

Irritated, I jumped into my truck. But for the first time in years I was excited for school.

I just hated that it was Alec's face that came into my head, Not Demetri's. I turned on the radio to distract me, and rolled my eyes as one of AD2's infamous songs began to play. Alec's voice was first. I only knew that because I'd seen the music video. I hated that while Demetri was the one irritating the crap out of me, Alec was the one I was curious about. It had to be the whole hard-to-get thing, not to mention he was brooding. Girls liked brooding. I got to school and tried to push the thoughts of the guys out of my head. Math. I needed to focus on math.

Chapter Seven

By the next Friday the news had been announced that the band AD2 was taking a much needed hiatus from touring, claiming the brothers were exhausted and spending time at their cottage in Oregon and attending school in order to bring some normalcy back into their lives.

It sounded super believable. I would have probably thought the story was legit. But Demetri made me doubt it. But what other purpose could there be behind them being here?

My mom was as reclusive as ever, and I was actually looking forward to going to Evan's party with Alec.

We ran together every morning. Demetri never said anything about it, but I wondered if it upset him.

Demetri followed me everywhere at school like a puppy dog. If he was trying to annoy me, it was working. Though it was more flattering than annoying. I got more glares from girls in those few days put together than I had in my entire life. Alec ignored me completely as if he was embarrassed to be seen in public with me. He was always glaring at people and hardly ever said two words unless spoken to.

The one time I approached him, he gave me a small smile and brushed me off. I wish I could say that I stopped running with him, but I couldn't help it. I was drawn to him. It seemed like the mornings were ours. We talked about music and his family. Never about his brother and never about school.

After a few weeks I was able to be seen in public with either guy and not freak out, meaning I could walk in a straight line and chew gum without choking. Demetri had warned me that his brother was different, that I needed to keep my distance, but I figured that was just jealousy talking. Not that I was anything to be jealous over. I mean, Demetri had kissed me. But he hadn't made a move since then. He joked around with me, carried my books everywhere, but that was the extent of it. Maybe he found me interesting, like some sort of pet he could watch and spend time with. Oh, my gosh! Was that what I was? A fish? Some sort of entertainment because he was curious about high school life and the real world?

I had two hours until the party and still hadn't decided what to wear.

My cell sang the familiar AD2 ringtone. Demetri had successfully hacked into my phone and changed all my ringtones to their band. I was too impressed to be upset.

"What's up, Alesha?"

"You're going tonight, right?" she asked excitedly.

"Um, yeah, I told you this morning."

"Oh." Long silence. "I forgot. Anyway, wanna get ready together?"

"Yeah, but Alesha, I don't really have anything here to wear—"

The line went dead. Well, that was Alesha for you.

Within minutes she was hauling a pile of clothes and a makeup tote through the door.

"Are we moving into Evan's?" I choked.

"No, silly, but it is a sleepover, so pack some cute

lingerie." She swatted me with her free hand after she put down the duffel. "You're already with Demetri, not that I can blame you. He's staked his claim repeatedly. First by kissing you on the cheek in the hallway and then again when he told every guy in the locker room that if they looked at you he'd castrate them. I swear, if peeing on you would mark his territory more, he'd do it."

I didn't know he'd been talking about me. I shifted uncomfortably. I hadn't ever really talked to Alesha about Demetri. It didn't feel right. Just because she thought we were an item didn't make it true. He hadn't made one move since the beach.

"Anyway…" She flicked a piece of hair away from her face. "Since he's taken, I'm going to go for the angry one."

"Alec." I clarified.

"Duh!" She pulled out a tight black dress. "Here you go!"

"Please tell me that is my pajamas." I grasped the small piece of fabric, already feeling my face flush with embarrassment.

"Nope, that's your dress." She moved behind me and tsked. "We should probably fix your hair too."

I lifted my hand to my hair. "What's wrong with it?"

"Way too flat." She grabbed a piece and grimaced as if I was somehow unclean, "We'll rat it, no biggie."

And just like that, I was turned from slave into Cinderella. That is, if Cinderella suddenly decided to become a prostitute.

"Absolutely not," I said, looking at my figure in the mirror. I didn't necessarily look bad, just cheap, and not at all like myself.

"Trust me, Demetri will die!" She clapped behind me. Alesha had low slung jeans and a short white off-the-shoulder shirt that barely covered half her chest.

"Not sure I wanna kill him, Alesha." I hadn't the heart to tell her I was actually going with Alec. She'd find out soon enough I guess.

"Crap!" She looked at her phone and hurriedly grabbed the rest of her clothes. "I gotta go, Evan forgot to get ice. I swear if that boy graduates high school I'm giving him a medal." She ran to the door then stopped and turned around. "And don't forget to pack your PJ's. Evan doesn't want anyone driving."

Great, add alcohol to another lists of firsts. I gave her a thumbs-up, but felt sick to my stomach with dread. I had always avoided Evan's parties like the plague. I'd seen first hand what those type of parties did to people, mainly what they did to Evan, since he always had the weekend shift and ended up showing up to work looking like he wanted to die a thousand deaths.

I looked at the shoes she left me. They were tall, intimidating, and pointy. I put them on and hobbled around the room as I tried to get my bearings. Finally, I looked at the finished product in the mirror. I guess it wasn't that bad. What at first looked like dark makeup, really only brought out my features more. She used soft shadows to make the color in my otherwise plain brown eyes pop. And she straightened my hair. It looked really shiny and bright, not dull like normal.

I added the lip-gloss she left me just in time for the doorbell to ring.

After two failed attempts to run down the stairs I quickly threw off the shoes and opened the door.

Alec was leaning against the frame, all six-foot-four of him. He wore a tight muscle-tee and a leather jacket like they were made for him. Add that to his jeans ripped in all the right places, and suddenly I was thankful Alesha put me in the dress.

His eyes widened for a brief second before he aggressively shrugged out of his jacket and draped it over my shoulders. "Wow."

"What?" Did I have lipstick on my teeth? Crap. I knew

this was a bad idea.

Alec hung his head. "The jacket's just making it worse. How is adding more clothes making it worse?" He cursed again and looked away.

"I can change."

"No!" His hands shot out to grasp my arms, the jacket slipped off and suddenly I was in his embrace.

His heavily lidded eyes gazed at my lips. With a sigh, he pulled his arms away and took a step back. "You ready to go?"

Shaken from our encounter, I could only nod and grab the shoes I had tossed at the foot of the stairs.

I grabbed my overnight bag and followed him to his SUV.

By now I knew he drove a brand new Lexus LS 570. The car smelled like expensive leather, and although I was happy to be going with him to Evan's party, I was still envious I wouldn't be able to drive the car.

"Stop lusting over my car, Nat." The darkness only aided in making Alec look more dangerous and handsome. Black wavy hair fell over his forehead. I wanted to brush it out of his eyes, but we didn't have that type of friendship where we were comfortable with touching each other in any capacity. Every time he accidently brushed my hand, or even my arm, he would jerk back as if I burned him or something. I wasn't sure if it meant that he was repulsed by me or felt the exact same electricity I did.

In fact, he was the perfect gentleman, which he proved again upon arrival at the party when he ran to my side and opened the car door.

"Are you for real?" I blurted.

"What?" He looked genuinely confused.

"You opened my door," I said dumbly.

Alec's eyebrows drew together as if he was trying to figure out why I was so amazed. "How else were you supposed to get out of the car?"

Well, when he put it that way.

"Nevermind," I muttered semi-irritated that he was being so nice to me. Why couldn't he be this nice at school? Why did he always keep his distance? It would be so much easier to forget about him if he would just be distant all the time. But no, he went around opening doors for girls and asked if they needed ice after a run, and even tied their shoes for them. Okay, so really, he just did those things for me, but still! Who did that to a complete stranger? A normal, boring, girl who lived in Seaside, Oregon?

Crap. I wanted to yell. Instead I gritted my teeth and followed Alec inside. The party was already crowded. Kids I hadn't seen in years suddenly came out of the woodwork. You know the type. The ones you could have sworn transferred or dropped out, and suddenly they're running around and talking to you like you're best friends.

Alec grasped my arm. His touch shocked me, and unfortunately caused me to trip right into his arms.

"You okay?" He righted me and grasped my shoulders looking intently into my eyes.

"Yeah, um..." His eyes were so green. For a minute I forgot to breathe, or at least it felt like it. His gaze never wavered as he waited for me to answer, I just wasn't sure I would be able to. Weren't high school boys supposed to be jerks? Players? Horny? Alec was none of those things. Indifferent, yes. But... "Just not used to heels, I guess," I finally managed.

"You made it!" Demetri came up behind me and squeezed my side, his hand dangerously close to my butt as he pulled me into a side hug and kissed my neck. What had once given me chills now left me a little irritated. Couldn't he see Alec and I were having a moment? Well, I was having a moment. Alec was probably waiting for me to stop having a seizure.

"Damn, you look sexy!" Demetri's nose went instantly

into my hair as he again nipped my neck. "Please tell me you're staying with me tonight."

I didn't answer. I couldn't. Not with Alec's gaze boring into mine the way it was. Helpless, I looked at Demetri. His blonde hair was sticking up all over the place, his blue eyes alive with amusement and excitement, but slightly glazed over.

"How much have you had to drink?" I asked.

"Enough to feel good, but not so much that I can't please you later, Babe." His mouth sloppily met mine. I fought the urge to push him back, but every time I was in his arms I felt wanted. I hated that I liked that feeling, but Demetri could have anyone, and for some reason he wanted me. He chose me.

When he stumbled back I glanced behind him and noticed that Alec had wandered off.

"Parties aren't really his scene," Demetri explained grabbing my hand. "He'd rather read a book, or go to a poetry slam, or whatever gay guys do."

My head jerked so fast I nearly fell over. "Gay?"

"Well, I have my suspicions," Demetri admitted, pulling me onto the dance floor. "Now come on, I've been waiting for you all night. Let's see those moves."

He twirled me a few times. I laughed because I couldn't help it. I liked it when Demetri was happy, and I had to admit I loved that girls were looking at me as if they wanted to stab me and steal my boyfriend.

Was he my boyfriend?

We danced for a while. Sweat formed at the base of my neck. I was so thirsty.

"Drinks?" Demetri nodded and grasped my hand.

He went to the punch bowl and filled our red cups to the rim. "Cheers."

"What are we celebrating?" I leaned in so he could hear me.

He took a big gulp of his drink. "I thought you knew?"

"Knew?"

Demetri placed the cup on the counter next to us and pulled me into his arms. Usually my head only met his shoulders, but with my heels I was eye-to-eye with his chin, big improvement.

"I want you to be my girlfriend."

And this is the part where any sane girl would look around the room for a hidden camera.

"Excuse me?" I said weakly.

"You. I want you." His lips found mine. My world tilted as he pushed me against the counter, his tongue licking the corner of my mouth before he slowly took a step back and gazed into my eyes. His look was predatory, hungry, as he swooped down and kissed me again. His hands slid beneath the straps of my dress and tugged down towards my bra. It was so sudden I could only respond with a moan. His control was gone. Never had he been so flippant with me, so aggressive. Panicking just slightly, I tried to push him away, get him to cool off. I still wasn't used to that type of attention and part of me still doubted what he said. After all, he looked somewhat wasted, and I could have sworn I saw him swallow some sort of pill with his beer earlier when we were dancing.

"Are you sure?" His large arms braced my body as he lifted me off the ground, his kiss sending an alarming if not, lustful thrill through my body.

"I'm sure," he whispered, pulling away and winking.

For some reason the satisfaction that was supposed to come at a time like this was absent. Instead, I felt… kind of sick. Maybe it was because I was dehydrated. I took a sip of the red cup and nearly spit the contents onto the floor.

"What is this?"

"Rum Punch." Demetri shrugged. "And I think a couple other things. Don't tell me you've never been to a party before, Nat."

"Fine, I won't tell you." I put the cup on the counter.

"What's with the crabby attitude?" He held me against his chest and kissed my neck. "Why don't we go outside and get some fresh air?"

I nodded. That was exactly what I needed. Fresh air. It was freakishly hot in Evan's house. Speaking of Evan. "Have you seen Evan?"

Demetri laughed. "Um yeah, he's currently wrapped up in Alesha's arms. Pretty sure he's going to swallow her lungs any time now." He pointed to the corner where Alesha was mauling one of my best friends.

"Right." I swallowed the panic I felt at not having anyone near me that I could really trust. I mean, how much did I really know Demetri? Enough to know that I was attracted to him despite warning bells chiming in my head every time he was near.

By the time we reached the front door, the room felt like it was spinning. Great, add a panic attack to my already awesome night.

Demetri stumbled slightly, forcing me to grab him so he could walk in a straight line. "Whoops!" He laughed and pushed open the screen door to the porch.

Evan's house was nestled a few blocks from the beach. His parents were never home. Everyone in Seaside knew he threw these parties. It just seemed like nobody cared. Sometimes the cops came by, but even then there were always bigger fish to fry in our sleepy town. So it wasn't ever a problem.

"Beach?" Demetri said breathlessly into my ear.

No. Absolutely not. Not with him drunk. With my luck he'd try to swim and I'd have to jump into the frigid water and save his sorry butt.

"Um, why don't we just walk around the block? I really don't want to be away from the party that long."

"Okay." He shrugged and fell into step beside me. "So,

you never said yes."

"To?"

He threw his head back and laughed, still unsteady on his feet. "Being my girlfriend. Damn, you're adorable."

I could have sworn I said yes, but then again, he had quickly kissed me and I'm a little fuzzy on what was being said, what with all the music and Demetri slobbering all over me.

"Why me, Demetri? You date movie stars. You date girls who look like supermodels. I guess I'm kind of confused. I mean, on top of all that, isn't this sorta fast? I mean, we've known each other for like two weeks."

Demetri stopped walking and leaned against the chain-link fence, folding his arms across his chest. "Baby, you want to see fast, I'll show you fast. This is the slowest I've gone in a relationship."

Right.

"Besides…" He pushed away from the fence and leaned down to kiss me. "I want you. I figure you're the type of girl that needs the big gestures. I mean, you're special. Not the type to spend the night in my bed without any sort of commitment."

"So you want to put a label on us in order to get me into bed with you?" I asked, suddenly furious.

"No!" He started laughing all over again shaking his head. "Seriously, you have to be like the cutest girl on the planet." He kissed my forehead. "Babe, if I wanted to be in your bed, I could have done it a week ago."

Was he calling me easy?

"Stop glaring." He kissed my cheek and grabbed my hand as we continued our walk. "What I'm saying, very horribly might I add, is that I really like you. You're different. Not like other girls. I want to do things right by you."

I exhaled. That was better.

His smile was wide and excited as he pulled me into a

side hug and kissed the side of my mouth "Do you like me too?"

"Of course I do!" I punched him playfully on the arm. "But I'm thinking you don't have trouble with the opposite sex. I mean, I do read the gossip magazines like everyone else."

His arm tensed on my shoulder. "You shouldn't read that crap."

"It's not like I believe any of it," I reassured him, looking into his eyes to convey the seriousness of my confession.

"Good." His smile had vanished. "It's just that, a lot of those gossip magazines have it all wrong about me. I mean, I'm not the man-whore they make me out to be."

"Really?" It was my turn to be serious.

He grinned. "Nat, I'm dead serious. I'm not that bad. I mean, I'm bad, don't get me wrong. I'm probably the worst sort of guy for you, but I'm selfish enough to ignore all the signs that say I'm wrong for you when all I want is to be with you."

"So first, I'm different, second I'm easy, and now you're ignoring your common sense to be with me? Wow, I actually believe you about the gossip magazines being wrong. No way do you have any sort of game, Demetri."

"Hey!" He put my head down between his arm and body so it was stuck underneath is arm in a headlock. "I've got plenty of game."

"Prove it!" My words were muffled by this shirt. He didn't smell like Alec. He smelled like peppermint and cigarettes. Did he smoke?

"Fine." He released me and stepped back. "Natalee." He took both my hands in his, gone was the smile. His eyes gazed intently into mine. "You are the most unique and beautiful girl I have ever had the pleasure of meeting. When I'm with you, you make me want to be a better man. You make me dream of things I never thought possible. But it's more than that — I want you. I want you so bad, that when you're not by my side, it hurts." He placed my hand over his heart then brought it up to his mouth to kiss it.

Dumbfounded, my mouth gaped open.

"I guess what I'm trying to say, " he continued, "Is that my heart hurts because it never knew what it was missing until now."

His eyes were glazed with unshed tears. Either he was the best actor in the known universe, or he was dead serious — or on drugs. Did drugs make you spout out romantic stuff like that? Mental note to look it up it when I got home.

"That was…" I gulped. "Beautiful, Demetri."

He winked. "I meant every word."

My heart picked up speed as he crushed his lips against mine, his hands got lost in my hair, sending shivers down to my toes.

"Stay with me tonight," he murmured again across my lips.

I nodded.

"Good." He stepped back. "Now let's go dance." His eyes were glazed as he tugged me into his arms and then pushed back. He was so hot and cold it was almost dizzying being with him. Did drugs do things like that to you? I mean, not that I was suspicious, but still. His mood swings were getting strange.

His hips did a seductive rock star move that I'm sure the kid's channel would censor, and I couldn't help but laugh.

"Whoa, easy, Tiger. Don't go moving like that all over the place. You could get random strangers pregnant."

His smile froze on his face. "That's not funny, Nat."

"I was kidding." I grabbed his hand but he pulled away.

"Whatever." He looked away and shoved his hands into his pockets. "Let's just get back."

What the heck did I just do? And why was he so upset? Geez! Talk about mood swings! Maybe he was just feeling the effects of all that drinking. He sure smelled like it, and I could have sworn I saw him pop something else in his mouth as we walked back toward the house. Ugh, I didn't know, but either way I was more than thrilled to be back inside. Demetri led me to the dance floor again. The dancing was different. He wasn't laughing anymore. Instead he was grinding against me, and to be honest, being kind of forceful about it.

"I… I need to use the bathroom!" I yelled in his ear.

He shrugged and walked toward the drinks.

Okay. Weird.

I had to crawl over at least thirty gyrating teenagers in order to find the bathroom, and when I did there were people making out in there.

Awesome.

I went to the upstairs bathroom and was relieved to find it empty.

Shutting the door, I leaned against it and exhaled. Did I really want to spend the night with him? Was his definition of spending the night and mine the same? Or was he expecting me to do things I knew I wasn't ready for?

Confused, I splashed water on my face, took care of my business, and ran back down the stairs. We needed to talk. I had to set boundaries, even if he made fun of me for it.

Chapter Eight

I skipped down the stairs, noticing that lots of people were already passing out. According to party rumors, Evan usually rented out the nice rooms to his close friends, meaning I probably got one of the guest rooms for the night. Everyone else had to camp in his huge backyard. Other people sometimes went to the beach and slept.

That rum punch must have been strong, because the party had been only going on for about three hours.

I walked back toward the dance floor, but a hand reached out to grab mine.

"Alec!" I yelled, half because I was frightened, half because I was excited.

"Hey." His eyes were dark, his mouth set in a grim line. "Maybe we should go."

"Are you sick?"

"Something like that." He looked away, a disgusted smirk spread across his face.

I nodded my head. "Okay, well… um, let me just go talk to Demetri first."

"Nat, don't." He grabbed my hand again, but I jerked

away from him. "Don't worry! It will just take a second."

Seriously. What was with these boys?

I pushed through the crowd of people to where I saw Demetri last. He wasn't on the dance floor. Confused, I walked to the drinks. And that's when I saw him.

Mauling a girl from the junior class. She was a known slut, on the cheerleading squad and absolutely hammered.

Demetri's hands were underneath her shirt, and she was pushing him against the wall. Clearly, he was participating.

Rage started pumping through me. I wasn't sure if I wanted to punch her or him. How dare he say all those things to me then go scam on some cheap skank! I fought the tears that were pooling in my eyes. The music was suddenly too loud, the people obnoxious. I fought my way through the crowds, away from Demetri, away from Alec. No doubt he was trying to warn me.

"Nat, stop." It was Alec. I'd recognize his cologne anywhere. His arms braced behind me, holding me steady as he half-lifted me into his arms and walked out the door.

He was silent as he unlocked the door to the car and gently put me in the passenger side. Once he started the car and pulled out of the driveway and headed back toward my house, he said, "You can cry now."

So I did. Weird, because I didn't even realize how upset I was until he gave me permission to mourn the fact that my boyfriend of five minutes had just been cheating on me in front of everyone.

I would seriously be a laughingstock at school later this week. Just another girl who had fallen for Demetri's charms.

Alec pulled the SUV into his driveway and wordlessly got out of the car and walked to my side. He opened the door and scooped me up into his arms. Alec carried me into his house totally silent.

My eyes felt puffy. I cursed Alesha for making me wear mascara. I probably looked like a possessed raccoon.

Alec gently placed me on the couch and flipped on the lights to the living room. My eyes took in the smooth buttery yellow couch he had set me on, the flat screen TV, all the pictures of him and Demetri, and the wide set windows looking out toward the beach.

It wasn't anything like my house. It was trendy but really comfortable, whereas my house felt sterile and lonely.

I suddenly cried harder, knowing I had to return to an empty house. My mom and dad had most likely gone out. It was date night, after all. The thought of being alone made me want to run back to Evan's party just so I could crash in one of his guest rooms.

I never did do well with being in the dark by myself.

"Here." I didn't even know Alec was in front of me. My eyes fell on a mug of something. I took it and sipped.

Tea. Crap. I had just made out with his brother and he was making me tea, in his house, and telling me it was okay to cry.

"Thank you," I mumbled.

Alec knelt in front of me. His thumbs wiped the remaining tears from my eyes. "I'm sorry, Nat. He's drunk. I know that's no excuse, believe me. But if he was in his right mind he would have never done that. I know he likes you."

I nodded numbly.

"Want me to beat him up for you?" Alec asked a deadpan look on his face.

"Would you?"

Alec nodded.

The idea did have merit.

"Maybe just a black eye."

"Done." He smiled and sat next to me on the couch.

I set the mug on the table and started to get up. "I should go home. I mean, it's getting late."

"Fine, but if you go home I'm going with you. Your choices are as follows. Stay with me, while I sleep on the floor guarding your virtue from my brother if he decides to track you down, or I'm crashing at your place. It's not safe for you to stay by yourself, Nat. Your parents are gone, right?" He ran his fingers through his hair. "Look, I know it's Seaside and not L.A. I just don't feel good with you being there by yourself. You should hang here for a while."

I nodded. "You don't have to do that, Alec."

"Yes. I do." He swallowed and looked away. "So, what will it be?"

I looked around me. It was so comfortable. How ironic that I would be more comfortable at a stranger's house than my own. "I guess we could stay here."

"Good, because I already ordered pizza."

I laughed. "When did you do that?"

"I have my ways. Apparently, there's an app for that."

I shook my head. "Always is."

He grinned then cleared his throat, his smile suddenly vanishing. "Are you going to be okay?"

"Of course." My answer was too fast and forced.

Alec's eyes narrowed.

I looked away. "I'll be fine. I promise."

"Says the raccoon," Alec muttered.

"Jerk!" I laughed and playfully pushed him away from me. "I knew I shouldn't have worn mascara."

"It's not like you need it anyways." Alec's blue eyes scanned me intently. "You have the thickest dark eyelashes I've ever seen. It's like you're waving every time you blink. Actually I'd like to think it's a greeting each time, 'Hey, Alec. How you doin, Alec?'"

I burst out laughing. "Oh my gosh! That's kinda creepy, Alec, and I'm pretty sure every time I see you I'm going to blink even harder, because I'll be thinking about it, and then people are going to think I have something in my eye."

"Oh, I hope so." He grinned and jumped up from the couch. "That would be entertaining for me."

"Yes, and it's all about you," I joked.

"No." He turned back to me and offered a warm smile. "It's about you."

My heart stopped beating. Awesome. *Breathe, Nat, breathe!* Finally, my mouth opened and I was able to suck in enough air so I wouldn't pass out on his couch. Unfortunately, the air was saturated with Alec. Seriously, the way he smelled did things to me. I'd never been the type of girl to fixate on cologne, but wow. It confused me, made me want to jump on him.

Maybe those two sips of rum punch messed with my head.

"So…" Alec politely ignored my second awkward moment that night. "Until the pizza gets here, what do you say we play some cards?"

"Cards? You play cards?"

"Um, yeah? What else do you think there is to do on tour busses?"

"Sing?" I offered.

"I think not." Alec sauntered to a drawer and pulled out a deck of cards and a pad of paper. "I take a vow of silence while I'm on the bus, saves my voice."

"A vow of silence?"

He nodded.

"How exactly does that work?"

He smirked and shrugged.

"Oh, very funny." I narrowed my eyes and ripped the deck of cards out of his hands. "So a vow of silence. So you're like a monk?"

"Sure." He smiled. "Just call me Ghandi."

"Was he a monk?"

"I have no idea. That's why I'm in school, to learn smart crap like that."

I laughed and shook my head. I loved this side of Alec. He was so funny and different. I cleared my throat, hoping it would clear my head as well. "So what game are we playing?"

"Go fish," Alec said without smiling.

"Seriously?"

"Oh, absolutely." Alec grinned and reached behind him revealing a giant pack of Swedish fish. "So, this is how it works, every time a player says go fish, you have to literally go fish, but you can't use your hands."

"What do I use?"

"Your mouth." He winked. "And you can't let your lips touch the counter, it has to be all teeth. Cheaters will be punished."

"You've played this before?"

"Oh, honey, if this was an Olympic sport I'd have more medals than Phelps."

"Crap." I quickly dealt the cards and so started the game.

Within ten minutes I had already eaten five Swedish fish and accidently touched the table with my lips twice. The punishment he spoke of was the other player licking the Swedish fish and placing it on the cheater's cheek. You had to stay that way until it fell off, and then you had to eat the fish.

Good thing he had a five pound bag, because with the way I was playing it was going to be gone.

After the first game, I had successfully eaten fifteen fish. Alec had four.

A knock sounded at the door. "Oh, that's the pizza." Alec shot out of his seat toward the door, then abruptly turned back. "No cheating!" He placed his cards farther away from me.

I was never one to listen and had always been a rebellious little girl. Plus, I had the biggest sugar high. I grasped his cards and swapped them so he would have to keep eating the fish.

By the time he came back, the smell of pizza filled the living room. My stomach growled.

"I knew you were hungry." Alec went into the kitchen

and returned with a couple plates and napkins. "You gotta eat before you go to a party, Nat. That's like Partying 101. Never drink on an empty stomach, kay? Promise me if you ever go to a party again and plan on drinking, that you will eat beforehand."

I nodded. "I promise, Mom."

"Thanks, sweetie." Alec patted my head and laughed.

It was so easy with him. It was like, oh gosh, I'm totally going to kill Stephenie Meyer and *Twilight*. It really was like breathing. Sorry Jacob and Bella, but it's true. And I'm sorry, but being with a werewolf would not be like breathing. It would be like dying.

It was unexpected and completely confusing. I didn't expect Alec to be so relaxed, or fun, or even protective for that matter. Alec moved casually around the kitchen and grabbed some forks for us. He was so normal. It was as if I was the most important thing in the world, the most important person in the room. Even though it was just us, his phone kept buzzing off the table. He never once looked at it.

When it rang for the tenth time, he threw it on the couch and stuffed a pillow over it.

We ate our pizza in silence. I attacked mine like a woman starved. I usually didn't eat junk food, but oh my gosh, the greasy cheese was like manna from heaven. "Thank you," I finally said after devouring three pieces.

He had five, so I didn't feel as bad.

"Anytime." He wiped his mouth with a napkin and took our plates back to the kitchen. "How about one more game?"

"You're on!" I giggled. Oh no, I'm giggling like a middle schooler. He's totally going to know I cheated.

"You cheated," he announced when he sat back down across from me.

I giggled. "No I didn't."

"You're giggling."

"I'm a girl!" I fired back.

His eyes narrowed. "Fine, I'll play. But if I lose, I'll know, Nat. I'll know."

"I'm not afraid of you."

He leaned across the table, his face inches from mine. "You should be."

Wait, were we still talking about the game?

My gaze fell to his lips, then flashed back to his eyes.

He jerked back and cleared his throat. "Do you have any sixes?"

"Go fish."

He glared and leaned over to pick the fish off the table, his lips grazing the little red gummy. I gulped, suddenly hot all over watching his tongue slip out of his mouth and attach itself to the fish. I'd never had that type of response to two guys before. It scared the crap out of me.

And, great. I'm jealous of a candy.

His lips never touched the counter. He ate the fish and grinned triumphantly. His grin, however, was short lived. Some ten fish later, he was losing horribly, and I still didn't have to eat any more fish.

"I think I may be sick," he announced before having to go fish again.

"Aw, too many fish? We can just call the game now. I mean, it's not like you're going to win."

He quickly picked up the fish and then spit it at me. Shocked, my mouth dropped open, then I reached into the bag and began pelting him with the fish.

"Ah!" He jumped out of his chair and tackled me to the floor, trying to force a handful of fish into my mouth.

I closed my eyes and shook my head back and forth. His weight nearly crushed me. There was no way I was getting out from underneath him.

And then, it was as if at the same time we realized what was happening. I slowly opened my eyes to see him staring at my mouth like a man starved.

My breath grew ragged as Alec's eyes dilated. He licked his lips and leaned down. I closed my eyes.

"Alec!" The voice jolted both of us away from one another. Alec cursed and helped me up. Demetri was walking through the door… well, stumbling and winding through the hallway was more like it. He was still smashed.

"I can't find Nat! I messed up! Where is she? Is she okay?" Demetri's words were slurring together. "Some guy told me I was making out with a chick that wasn't Nat. I didn't know, Dude. Where the hell is she?" This was not the time or place to have this discussion, especially considering Demetri was drunker than a skunk.

He tumbled into the living room, still not looking in my direction. He smelled like cigarettes and whiskey. "Where's she, man?"

I cleared my throat.

"Natalee!" Demetri opened his arms, I stepped back.

"Just sleep it off, bro." Alec tried to pull his brother back toward the stairs, but Demetri fought him.

"No! Natalee, I'm so sorry, Babe. I'm so sorry!" He fell to his knees and looked like he was ready to cry. "It wasn't what you think! I'm so drunk — she had blonde hair, I thought she was you!"

I knew it was stupid to argue with a drunk person, but I couldn't help myself. "Really? And when you found out you were wrong you decided to do what? Kiss her back?"

"I'm so sorry!" He ignored my question, still on his hands and knees.

"Sleep it off, Demetri." Alec moved to grab his brother, but Demetri jerked away then took an awkward swing at him, throwing himself off balance even more. He stumbled and rocked back on his heels.

"A promise is a promise," Alec muttered before punching his brother directly in the eye.

Demetri cursed as he tumbled to the ground and

promptly passed out.

I was frozen in place.

"Is he okay?"

Alec shrugged. "Besides having a headache and the black eye I promised, yeah, he'll be fine."

I nodded, still in shock.

"Come on." Alec held out his hand. "Let's go upstairs and get you into bed. I don't care what you say. I'm sleeping on your floor just in case the drunk wakes up and decides to apologize again."

"Okay." I felt bad leaving Demetri on the floor. Alec noticed me staring and rolled his eyes, moved back to him, and lifted Demetri, depositing him on the couch.

"Happy?" he asked.

"Yes." Alec's mood had changed again, it wasn't as lighthearted. More irritated and crazy protective.

I followed him down the dimly lit hall. There were at least ten doors that led into different rooms. He took me to the last room and opened the door, allowing me to go first.

I gulped.

It was his room. It had to be. I was almost alarmed at how clean it was. Didn't boy rooms usually smell bad?

His windows were open, so the curtains were blowing in the slight breeze. It smelled like Alec and the ocean. I decided it was my favorite smell, even more so than his cologne by itself, because it was a mixture of him and home.

The room was huge and had a bathroom off the side of it. His large bed was near the windows and seemed menacing. "I'll just grab you some sweats to sleep in, kay?" Alec scratched the back of his head then went to a walk-in closet and turned on the lights. His closet was bigger than my room.

He reached into a dresser and searched. Within seconds he was tossing me a t-shirt and sweats. "Will these work?"

"Yeah, they're fine." I grabbed them.

We stared silently at one another for a minute or two.

I shifted on my feet and Alec quickly looked down at the floor. "Do you want to shower?"

"Kind of, I mean, if that's okay. If not, it's totally fine. I can just go to sleep and—"

"Nat, stop talking so fast, you're making me nervous."

Right I'm making *him* nervous.

"I'll just sit out here and read for a bit. There's fresh towels hanging up, and you can use whatever's in the shower." He stretched his arms above his head, giving me a spectacular view of the lower part of his abs and the low slung jeans on the V of his hips.

I couldn't really speak. I quickly turned around, and my face met the wall. I was an inch away from chipping my tooth.

"Careful." I heard him chuckle behind me. Jerk.

I felt a blush spread from my face all the way down to my toes. I escaped into the bathroom and shut the door behind me.

Should I lock it?

No, he was a perfect gentleman, he wouldn't do anything. Unlike his brother, who would probably find some silly excuse to be in the bathroom at the exact same time.

They were so different.

My original judgment of them had been way off base.

I thought Alec was the brooding weird one and Demetri the bad boy masquerading as an angel, though their looks proved otherwise.

Apparently just because a guy glares and has dark features, doesn't make him the bad guy. Just like dimples and an easy smile don't automatically make him an angel.

I sighed and turned on the water.

Chapter Nine

It was a rain shower. The type you see on TV and at expensive hotels. I stood underneath it and immediately felt the stress leave my body as I closed my eyes.

The shower was scary clean.

As in, there's no way he actually showers in it.

But his body wash looked half used as well as his shampoo. I lathered my hair in the spicy scent and smiled. It smelled like him.

I was a girl obsessed.

The body wash was filled with tea tree oil. By the time I stepped out of the shower my skin was so soft I decided right then and there that I was going to go shopping and purchase everything I just used.

The bathroom was a little steamy so I couldn't see my reflection in the mirror. I looked around for some sort of face wash and finally settled on some store bought brand that looked expensive.

It smelled like a boy too, but it felt good against my face.

I dried off, and threw on the sweats. They were huge on me, but at least I felt more comfortable than I had before in the tiny dress and high heels.

I opened the door just in time to see Alec take his shirt off. I told my mouth to close, but it was pointless.

His body was muscled in all the right places, not an ounce of fat on him. A large angel wing tattoo spread across his right shoulder and part of his collarbone, another one was on his stomach. His one arm had a half-sleeve of different markings. Curious, I stepped forward. He still hadn't seen me.

I think I scared him as much as I scared myself when I reached out and touched his skin.

"Crap!" he yelled. "Sorry, Nat, I was lost in thought. Didn't see you." His breath smelled like peppermint.

I shook my head. "What does this mean?" I touched the foreign writing on his collarbone and traced it until it met another smaller tattoo near his stomach. It was a pair of hands holding a heart. He flinched as if my touch hurt him.

The tattoo wasn't in English. It spread across his chest and ran into the design on his right shoulder.

His eyes looked sad as he looked away. "It means my heart will be yours forever."

"Why did you get it?"

He jerked away and looked down. "For my son."

"You have a son?" I was so shocked I didn't know what to do. How did I not know this? I hadn't seen anything about it on the gossip sites.

"Had a son. I had a son, Nat. He died." Alec stepped away from me and went into the bathroom slamming the door behind him.

I wanted to cry.

Cry for Alec and the hurt expression in his face, and for the child that no longer had life. I hadn't lost anyone before. I couldn't imagine the depth of despair it would be for a parent to lose a child, especially a teen parent. You would feel so helpless.

I sighed and climbed into his huge bed.

Within minutes Alec came out of the bathroom. He turned off the lights and grabbed some pillows and a blanket from the foot of the bed.

He didn't say a word.

"Alec," I whispered.

"Yeah?" His voice was hoarse.

"I'm sorry."

He sighed. "Nat, you didn't know. It's fine."

"Alec," my voice cracked.

"Nat? Are you crying?"

It was too dark to see, but the bed heaved under the pressure of Alec sitting next to me. I could see the outline of his body from the moonlight as my eyes adjusted to the dark. He was wearing shorts, but no shirt.

"Maybe," I answered. I couldn't explain my behavior. I was crying over someone I didn't even know.

"Why? Is something wrong? Tell me what's wrong? Is this about Demetri?" His breath was hot on my face.

I shivered.

"Are you cold?" He grabbed a blanket and threw it over me. Great, now I was going to sweat to death.

"I don't mean to cry, Alec. It's just. I've never lost anyone before, and to think of losing a part of you, a child. I just. I don't know. I'm just so sorry it makes my heart hurt to think about it." I reached out and touched his arm. This time he didn't flinch.

"Nobody's ever said that to me." His breathing was slow and calculated. "I mean, nobody knew but Demetri, and as you can see he deals with problems a little differently than I do."

I nodded even though I knew he couldn't see me. "What was his name?"

"Benjamin."

"How did he die?"

Alec sighed then slowly lay down on the bed next to me

on top of the covers. "It was my fault."

"How was his death your fault?"

Alec laughed bitterly. "There's a lot you don't know about me, Nat. I haven't always been so… boring."

"Oh."

"Yeah, oh," Alec repeated. "Let's just say his mother was a one night stand, but the minute I found out she was pregnant I told her I would help out. We paid her off, to keep it out of the media. It was right when we started getting really big."

"Ah, the infamous MTV concert."

Alec laughed softly. "Yes, the MTV concert. We signed with a bigger record label and had to stay out of trouble. I was only sixteen."

Ouch.

"So how was it your fault?"

Alec was silent for a few minutes. "Benjamin's mom was in rehab, Nat. She was so messed up, but I was so busy and things were happening so fast for us, that I didn't really pay attention to her when she got out. I told her I'd visit her, but had to keep canceling when they added more cities to our concert tour."

The only sound in the room was that of my own breathing and his.

"The night we found out we were nominated for a few Grammys, Benjamin's mom got in a car accident. Both her and Benjamin were killed on impact."

Tears flowed freely down my cheeks. I blindly searched for his hand and held it.

He pulled me as close as he could with the blankets covering me and sighed. "Please Nat, please don't tell anyone. You don't understand. Nobody knows this. I don't want my son's picture thrown around TV. I don't want him remembered as some bastard child by a punk rock star."

"Nobody would think that."

"Yes…" He sighed heavily. "They would. And I refuse to let that happen."

His story explained a lot. Why he was so distant, so protective. So in control of everything in his world.

"Thanks for telling me," I said.

"Well, it's not every day a girl cries over a little boy she didn't even know."

"I'm crying for you too, Alec."

He shuddered. "Thanks, Nat. That means more to me than you'll ever know." His lips found my forehead in a chaste kiss. "Now, get some sleep before my jerk of a brother wakes up and tries to break the door down."

"Okay." I wanted him to stay with me so badly. I wanted to fall asleep in his arms, his breath mingled with mine. He was like a drug, an addiction I was slowly needing more and more of.

Each of the brothers had their demons. Which left me to wonder where I fit in the picture. It made all my insecurities flare to life. What the heck were they doing even paying attention to me? I was nothing — nobody. My own parents seemed uninterested in me. It was nice to have people care about me, even if they were confused rock stars, but I couldn't help but wonder if I was somehow stepping out onto a ledge without any way to escape except jumping.

The last picture in my head before my eyes grew heavy was of a little boy with bright blue eyes, a little boy who looked like Alec.

Chapter Ten

I woke to the smell of fresh coffee.

With my eyes still closed I moaned and stretched across the pillows.

"You have no idea how much you affect me when you do that," Demetri said.

My eyes flashed open.

He looked like a truck ran over him.

He hadn't showered or done anything. Purple and blue bruises decorated the side of his eye and his cheekbone.

I hadn't realized Alec hit him so hard. Immediately my eyes went to the floor. "He's downstairs making breakfast. He said he'd give me some time to talk to you but that if I make you cry I have to drown myself in the ocean."

I nodded. "I agree to those terms."

"Ouch." Demetri chuckled and looked away. "I don't even know what to say, Nat. Sorry just seems lame. I'm an ass sounds a little better, but I just don't know what to say."

He plopped down onto the bed and ran his hands through his messy blonde hair. "I really like you. I've never liked a girl as much as I like you. I meant everything I said last night. I want to be with you."

"And every other girl at Seaside," I added, suddenly feeling the hurt and betrayal of last night wash over me.

"No!" He grasped my hands and kissed them. "You don't understand. I only want you. I know I seem like a screw up, and that's because I am. I can't believe I'm saying this. I think you're the forever girl. The one you bring home to your parents, the one you spend Christmas with, the one you have children with. You're that girl, Nat."

"I don't know how to respond to that."

Demetri sighed. "I don't expect you to forgive me, Nat. What I did was childish and stupid. I got drunk at a party and made out with a complete stranger just because she was in front of me. I don't even remember who it was. I only know she had blonde hair. I really did think she was you, but when I noticed she wasn't, I was too drunk too care."

"Well, at least you're honest."

"Honesty sucks." He exhaled and looked away. "Nat, I want to be with you. Let me earn your trust again. Let me be the guy I've always wanted to be. I want to be that guy for you."

Having a guy say that was like crack for a girl. "I can't save you, Demetri."

"I don't want you to. I just want you by my side as inspiration when I save myself."

Crap.

I felt my guard crumbling as his blue eyes glazed over with unshed tears. "Please, Nat."

Demetri reached out and cupped my chin. His touch was warm, gentle, not at all like last night. Desire flared in his eyes, so different from Alec.

I would never have Alec.

But Demetri. He needed me, and part of me craved that feeling. To be needed, wanted. I'd never experienced anything like it before. My parents loved me, but they functioned apart from me.

"Help me be better. I need you in my life, Nat. You're like my sunshine, my air. I can't explain it, I just know I'm lost without you." He kissed my cheek.

"Don't make me regret this, Demetri."

A smile spread across his face. "Really?"

I nodded.

"Do you want breakfast?" He pushed away from the bed.

"I'm starving."

Demetri chuckled and pushed the covers back, lifting me into his arms. "I bet you are. Though a little bird told me you ate quite a bit of Swedish fish last night."

"I'm going to kill Alec!" I yelled.

Demetri threw his head back and laughed. "I should have warned you how he plays Go Fish."

"He's an animal!" I yelled as Demetri carried me down the stairs. I rolled my eyes towards the ceiling. Really, it wasn't as if I was on my death bed or something, but I had to admit, it was kind of nice to be in his arms.

Though my treacherous body couldn't help but remind me that it was Alec's arms that had rescued me last night. I gulped.

"Heard that!" Alec fired back from the kitchen.

I smiled, and then my heart dropped to my knees. What was I doing? I looked at Demetri, his blinding smile was for me, only me. But what about Alec? Was I imagining a connection with us?

Demetri placed me on my feet. I walked timidly into the kitchen. Alec was cooking eggs and bacon. Orange juice and coffee were already laid out on the counter.

"Morning, sleepy head. Did you know you snore?" Alec said, not looking a way from the skillet.

"I do not!"

"Do to," the boys said in unison.

"You were drunk!" I punched Demetri.

"Drunk, sweetheart, not deaf."

I glared.

"She's crazy when she's hungry," Demetri said under his breath as he quickly grabbed a plate and began piling it with food.

I willed Alec to turn around. But he didn't.

Finally, after a few minutes in which I'm sure I lost brain cells trying to use telepathy to get the man to look at me, he turned.

Everything seemed normal.

He gave a small smile and went to the fridge. "I'm gonna go for a run. I'll see you guys later."

And just like that he was gone.

"Is he okay?" I nudged Demetri who was eating like he hadn't seen food in days.

"Who? Alec? Of course, he's fine. Why wouldn't he be okay?"

"I don't know." I nibbled my lower lip. "Did you guys talk this morning?"

"Yeah." Demetri stopped shoveling food into his mouth and took a drink of orange juice. "He told me I was an ass, and that I was going to lose the best girl in the world if I didn't get up to the room and grovel. Naturally, I knew all that before he mentioned it, but still."

Breakfast sat like a stone in my belly. So Alec had encouraged me and Demetri? Clearly I had read every signal wrong. All the protective gestures and weird sensually charged moments. It was all in my head. Alec didn't want me. Demetri did.

Foolishly, I thought if I lingered a bit that Alec would return from his run. An hour later he still wasn't back.

"I should go," I said to Demetri as he finished up the last of the breakfast dishes.

"Stay." He placed the wet dish on the counter and walked around to pull me into his arms. His kiss was gentle. I liked this side of him so much better than last night. I could almost believe he was the good guy, the white knight. The guy he said he wanted to be.

"I can't." I shook my head even as he kissed my cheek and my nose.

"Why?"

"Because!" I pushed away a grin spreading across my face at his confusion. He really was used to getting everything he wanted. "I have a ton of homework and some of us have to work for a living."

"I work."

I tilted my head to the side. "According to you, you're taking a much needed break right now."

"True, but I still work."

"Fine, you work, but that doesn't change anything. I still have to go to my part-time job, and I have to fit in a run sometime today and do homework." I huffed and crossed my arms. The thought of everything I needed to accomplish that day actually stressed me out a bit. My eyes flickered to the clock. It was already ten. I had to be at the taffy store in two hours.

"Fine," Demetri grumbled. "Where do you work?"

"Seaside Taffy."

Demetri smirked. "Do you wear cute little outfits and give out free samples?"

I rolled my eyes. "This conversation is going downhill fast."

"Always." He chuckled. "Sorry, no more sexual innuendos. Okay, go get ready for work, do your run, and we can hang out later."

I nodded. "Aw, you're learning so fast."

"Do I get rewarded for good behavior?"

"And then he defaults."

"Crap." Demetri crossed his arms and pouted. He looked so innocent and sexy that I gave in. I leaned up on my tiptoes and kissed him firmly across the mouth.

Immediately he parted his lips, his mouth tasted like oranges. Shockingly he kept his hands at his sides.

He pulled back. "You taste good."

"So do you."

We stared at each other for a while. His eyes glanced at my mouth. With a sigh I stepped back. "I'll text you, 'kay?"

He nodded as I gave him a wave and ran out the door.

Weird how much things could change in twenty-four hours.

I looked in vain down the path. Alec was nowhere to be found. He probably took another route.

****

I cursed Alec for making such a good breakfast. My run was not going as planned. I kept getting side-aches. The food was like a giant boulder in my stomach.

I got to mile three and turned around. The stretch ahead of me might as well have been Everest for how ready my body felt to run it.

I grabbed my iPod and switched to a different mix.

The list that said *Crush.*

It brought a smile to my face when the techno beat of AD2 started playing in my ears. Before, when I listened to their music I could never tell which brother was singing. Now, it was impossible not to tell. Alec had the deeper voice of the two, he usually sang the melody — he carried the song.

Demetri's voice was slightly higher. It sounded almost too perfect, kind of like the guy from Rascal Flatts. He usually did the bridges and verses.

But when they sang together, their harmony was perfect. Their music was the kind that any age liked. Their concerts were filled with girls between the ages of eight and eighty.

The fourth mile back went fast. The fifth was even faster,

and I was already on my sixth AD2 song when I stumbled.

I looked down. Ugh, stupid shoelaces. I really needed to double knot them, but I was in such a hurry to get my run in before work that I forgot.

"Nat, you should really invest in lessons on how not to trip," Alec's voice called from behind me.

I tugged my earphones out and turned around.

Sweat poured down his body. He had taken off his shirt at some point, and it was clenched in his right hand, leaving his ridiculous six-pack bare. It didn't help that his sweat seemed to glisten on his chest in the sun.

"What, did you just run a marathon or something?" I joked.

"Nah."

I nodded.

"A half marathon."

"I feel very inadequate," I mumbled, kicking a rock from my shoe.

"As you should." Alec knelt down and tied my shoe very tight, as if I was in kindergarten and had a habit of tripping over shoelaces. Well, I guess the tripping part was fairly accurate.

"So, things are good?" Alec asked, not meeting my eyes but looking at the beach instead.

"I guess." I shrugged. "Demetri said you talked to him."

"He did?" Alec turned to me, he looked surprised.

"Yeah." This was the part where he's supposed to get the hint and expand on the topic. But of course, he was a guy so he just shrugged.

"So…" I gulped. "I have to work today, but I think we're hanging out tonight if you want to join us."

"Did you just invite me out on your date?"

"It's not a date," I said quickly.

"Trust me." He grinned bitterly. "It's a date. But yeah, I actually have some stuff going on tonight. You guys have fun though, okay?"

"Okay." I swallowed the lump in my throat. Rejection did not feel good, not when it came from Alec.

"Nat?"

My head snapped up.

"I'm happy for you."

Tears welled in my eyes. "Thanks, Alec. That means a lot."

He nodded and put his earphones back in. "Try not to trip on the last mile home."

"Very funny," I grumbled and took off like a crazy person back toward the house. I only had forty five minutes to get ready for work.

I hated that the only thing I could conjure up in my mind was the look on Alec's face when we talked.

We were back where we started. The casual friends who joked around but shared nothing. It shouldn't matter. After all, I wasn't anything to him. I was just his friend. His brother's girlfriend.

Chapter Eleven

Work was busy.

It seemed like everyone and their mom had decided to come into Seaside for the weekend. I was handling the crowds fine until a mom with three screaming kids walked in. The children began running in circles and testing every flavor of salt water taffy as if it was free.

"Evan." I elbowed him. He still looked hung over from the night before. He was holding his head in his hands and moaning.

"Why. Do. Children. Exist?" His teeth were clenched.

I would have laughed if I didn't feel so bad for him. He said his head hurt so bad he wanted to die this morning. That's what he gets for underage drinking. I took it upon myself to slam the doors more often during our shift.

But the little kids were making my job easy — he was miserable.

"Make it stop, please make it stop." Evan drank from his bottled water and glared at the mother.

I wouldn't be surprised if she disappeared on the spot.

"Evan, here." I gave him some more aspirin and set about

cleaning the counter. Seaside Taffy was one of the largest taffy stores in the city. It had every flavor you could possibly think of, including some that didn't seem like they should be edible. Who wants to eat a grass flavored taffy? Or buttered popcorn?

We also served ice cream and caramel apples. Evan was usually in charge of the candy while I helped serve the other food. But today he just sat like a bump on the log.

"Seriously, Evan, I need help." I seethed two hours later when the line grew so long, it reached out the door and down the sidewalk.

Evan said something under his breath, but finally moved to the register and began taking people's money.

"Is it true?" A girl gushed to Evan.

"That your voice is very high pitched?" Evan offered. "I'm afraid so."

"Evan." I nudged him. "Sorry, sweetie, is what true?"

"That like, the band AD2 is staying here in Seaside and going to school?"

"Yup," Evan answered quickly. "Now what can we get you girls?"

They were in middle school and knew the art of distraction too well to allow us to manipulate them.

"So," the girl in pigtails said, jutting out her hip. "You guys look old."

Evan's grip tightened on the register. "Listen, you—"

"Yup, we're old! You're right!" I smiled wildly. "But girls, there's a line, we need to grab your order, okay?"

"Fine," they grumbled in unison.

When I handed them their caramel apples, the pig-tailed girl whipped around. "Since you're old and in high school, do you like know the guys?"

"Do I look like the type of girl a rock star would talk to?" I countered.

They tilted their heads, taking in my candy-striped uniform complete with white visor and shook their heads.

Awesome.

"Oh, I don't know. I'd talk to you, you know, if I was a rock star," a voice said to my left. I turned and immediately wanted to die.

Demetri was leaning against the ice cream counter. His muscled arms protruding out of a tight gray T-shirt that was half-tucked into low-slung designer jeans.

"Nice visor." This from the guy who has more female admirers than most movie stars.

I nodded.

The girls who had just been rapidly firing questions at me and Evan were shocked into silence.

"To answer your question," Demetri said, looking between the two of them, "This girl is the exact type of girl I would hang out with. I may even kiss her today. That is, if she lets me." He winked at the two girls.

I was convinced I would have to do CPR. Were they even breathing?

Finally the one vocal girl piped up, "Can we have your autograph?"

"Sure." Demetri pulled a marker out of his pocket and signed a few napkins for the girls before sending them on their way. My, he's prepared.

"Thank God." Evan looked at Demetri. "I couldn't handle any more of their shrieking or questions."

"Anytime." Demetri nodded at Evan than looked at me. "So, you're off in an hour right?"

"Yup." I ignored the weird looks from customers as well as the shrieks from other girls who had just discovered that the D from AD2 was currently having a conversation in Seaside Taffy with the shop girl.

"Cool. I have plans for you, Nat." His eyes did that thing were they magically get darker and close just slightly, making him look sexier than should be legal.

"Okay." It was the only thing I could say. The crowds

were getting ridiculous. "Hey, Demetri?"

He turned around.

"Take care of some of this for us?" I pleaded.

He threw his head back and laughed. "Fine, but you owe me!"

"I love him," Evan announced. "I'm not gay, but right now I love him. If he can take all the females and loud people away from here, I may just kiss him."

I rolled my eyes at Evan and laughed as Demetri left the store and signed autographs on his way. Just as I expected, once people noticed he was signing autographs, the crowds dwindled.

Evan looked around the empty store. "He's a god among men."

"Don't tell him that, he's cocky enough."

"I'd be cocky too if women threw their panties at me."

"Are you still drunk?"

A few seconds went by and then. "Maybe."

By the time my shift was over, my feet hurt, and I could feel a headache coming on, probably from all the stress.

I waved goodbye at Evan and grabbed my purse. I probably smelled like taffy and germy little kids, but I didn't care. I was just so excited that my shift was over. The bell chimed as I went out into the breeze.

And there was Demetri, leaning against a killer Mercedes CL 600. It was black. Figures.

"Nice ride." I suddenly felt very, very inadequate. Why the heck were these two guys paying me any attention?

He shrugged. "It gets me from A to B."

I'll bet it gets him to C too, but I kept my mouth shut. He was obviously proud of his car. I liked it. I mean, it cost more than most people's houses, but my mind flashed to Alec's car. It seemed less… I don't know, maybe less of a status thing? It was probably my imagination and I was tired.

"Your carriage awaits." Demetri opened the door and

ushered me in.

"But my truck." I pointed at my sad cheap truck and again wanted to disappear.

"I've already taken care of it. Keys." He held out his hand. I dug through my purse and handed them over.

He walked over to the truck and put the keys under the floor mat. "Alec said he'd take a run into town and drive it back to your place."

"Oh." Why did the brother who has no interest in me have to be so nice again? It confused me.

"Hop in."

The car smelled heavenly. A mixture of vanilla and leather. Wood paneling covered most of the dash. I've never sat in anything like it. I mean, my parents were well off, but we weren't loaded like this. This was beyond anything I'd ever seen.

I was so horribly out of my league it was almost depressing.

"So, dinner?" Demetri asked once he started the car and drove away from the curb.

"You don't mind that I'm dressed like this?" I pointed down to my clothes.

"It's kind of hot," he admitted. "Put the visor back on, Nat."

I laughed and crossed my arms. "Jerk."

"Aw, come on, babe, I'm kidding. I like the visor. Put it on one more time, just once."

I stuck out my tongue but put it on anyways.

He laughed and parked in front of Owen's, one of the nicer restaurants in Seaside.

I threw off my visor and tried to fluff my hair. At least I didn't have my apron on, but it didn't help that my outfit looked like something a person would wear for Halloween. I really was dressed as a candy-striper. The owner of the taffy shop thought it was funny and cute.

This was me not amused.

Demetri opened the door for me and ushered me in. The restaurant wasn't very crowded.

The hostess gave me a once over then smirked and looked back down at her table.

"Excuse me," Demetri said smoothly. "My girlfriend and I have reservations."

The lady didn't look up. "What name?"

"Demetri Daniels."

The hostess's hand began to shake. She gulped, then slowly looked up to meet Demetri's gaze.

"R-right away, Mr. Daniels." Her face flushed red and I was instantly pleased that he stood up for me. At least I think that's what he was doing.

The hostess led us to a far corner of the restaurant.

"If there is anything, anything at all, I can get for you two—"

"Wine," Demetri interrupted. "A house red, perhaps a Malbec?"

"Right away." The girl practically tripped over herself.

"Demetri, we're underage."

He shrugged. "I'm famous. They never card me. Trust me. They'll do anything for my business, including serving alcohol to minors. I mean, look at this place. It's kinda dead right now. Give it an hour."

The waitress returned with the wine and gave him an overly obvious wink as she uncorked the bottle. I refused the drink. Concern washed over me as Demetri engaged in conversation and nearly finished the entire bottle.

He sure could talk a lot about himself. Not that I minded, he was interesting, but still. He hadn't even asked about my day.

I yawned. I suddenly felt flush and exhausted.

Demetri ignored my yawn and obvious signs of exhaustion and kept talking. I hated his haughty attitude almost as much as I hated that he was right. Within an hour the restaurant was packed. It was so loud we almost couldn't have a conversation. It also didn't help that people kept approaching our table. I just wanted them to go away. This was not how I thought our date was going to go.

Demetri never ignored his fans.

But he ignored me.

The entire night.

Finally after dessert was served, I was ready to go.

Demetri was deep in conversation with a young girl who had just walked up and asked for an autograph. She couldn't be any older than me, and I was instantly jealous. She was flirting with my boyfriend. *My* boyfriend.

Just as I was about to open my mouth and most likely make a fool of myself, Demetri reached out and grabbed my hand.

A shiver of pleasure ran through me as the girl backed off and glared, then finally left.

"Sorry," Demetri apologized. "I didn't know it would get this out of hand."

"You're one of the biggest rock stars on the planet, and you didn't think it would get out of hand?" Was he for real?

He at least looked sheepish when he shrugged. "Sorry, it's never this bad in L.A. I mean, people usually give us our privacy. I can go to Starbucks and not be stalked."

"If you haven't noticed, the most exciting thing in Seaside is the ocean and the fact that we actually have a Starbucks. Of course people are going to freak out." I was kind of angry and tired. I needed to stop taking it out on him. It wasn't his fault.

Demetri cursed. "You're right, Nat. I'm sorry. Forgive me?" His smile immediately disarmed me.

I shrugged. "Fine, but no more ignoring me on our date."

"I promise a date will never be like that again."

"Why? Are we going to stay inside and become reclusive?"

Demetri grabbed my hand and kissed it. "No, the record company is sending over some bodyguards."

Suddenly everything felt very real. "Um, is that necessary?"

"We got a few death threats yesterday." He shrugged. "Nothing out of the ordinary, but you know, you should always be careful."

Feeling a little alarmed, I could only stare at him. On what planet was that normal? I was silent as he paid the check and led me out to the car.

Fans were bustling outside the restaurant just as much as inside. Utterly exhausted, I just wanted him to take me home.

"Let's go." Demetri strategically led me through the crowds. To say I was freaked out would be an understatement. I mean, he just told me he gets death threats and I can't even see the street right now.

"Demetri! Is that your girlfriend? Who is that?" A girl shouted, and then a camera flashed.

Demetri's hand tightened in mine, and then in one swift movement he pinned me against the car and kissed me.

When he pulled away I opened my eyes to at least forty phones pointed at us.

"Guess so." He nuzzled my hair, then tucked a few pieces behind my ear.

I think people were so excited and shocked, they didn't even realize we were hurrying to get into the car.

"Are you sure you can drive?" I asked. My throat was starting to feel achy and sore.

He laughed. "I've driven in worse situations."

"I mean the alcohol."

"So did I," he shrugged and started the engine. I should have said something more, or at least been more aggressive about him not driving, but I was so freaked out by all the people.

He sped down the road and turned the corner, then

finally opened his mouth to speak. "Sorry, did I hurt you?" He motioned to my mouth and arm that he had grabbed while kissing the crap out of me outside.

"No." I shook my head. "You shocked me a bit though. Why'd you do that?"

"Damn." Demetri hit the steering wheel.

"What?" I froze.

"We're being followed. I knew it was only a matter of time. It's just… We didn't think it would get this crazy here. I mean, it is Seaside."

"And again, need I remind you that we have computers?" Exasperated, I leaned against the door and closed my eyes.

"I'll drive around the block a few times to lose them, then we can go home, okay?"

I'm not sure if I said okay or nodded or what. My eyes felt so heavy. I had to close them. It was as if someone had drugged me. Maybe I should have been smarter about trying to do so much in one day.

With a yawn, I curled up in my seat and fell asleep.

Chapter Twelve

"What did you do to her?" Alec yelled. He never yelled. Why was he yelling? And why couldn't I open my eyes? I moaned and immediately a cool compress was pressed to my head. I shivered.

"I kissed her! That's it! We went to dinner and she fell asleep in the car!" Demetri cursed. "Geez, what, you think I drugged her or something?"

"Wouldn't be the first time," Alec grumbled.

"What the hell!" Demetri laughed. "Are you kidding me? Seriously? You're going to bring that up now of all times?"

Alec cursed. I felt his hand on my face. "Can you hear me, Nat?"

I moaned again and tried to pull away from him.

"We'll just take her home. She can sleep it off. She's probably sick," Demetri said a lot more calm now.

"No, we can't." Alec was stern. "Her dad and mom decided to extend their date night to a date weekend. They won't be back until tomorrow night. They kept leaving her messages but her cell phone must have died. Nat's mom knew you guys were out, so she left a message with me before they took off. They're gone."

"So?"

Alec's hand left my forehead. "So, if we leave her at her house and she's this sick, what do you think is going to happen to her? She's burning up."

"Oh." Demetri was quiet for a few minutes. "Does that mean she has a fever?"

"Just, go get some ibuprofen, Demetri."

"Fine." The door slammed behind him. It echoed in my ears making my head pound harder. I focused on opening my eyes and was rewarded greatly for my strain.

Alec was hovering over me, concern marked his features. "Nat, are you okay?"

"I think so." My voice was heavy and groggy. I felt emotional, like I wanted to cry. I wanted my mom. But she wasn't there. All I had were two rock stars, one who wanted to drop me off at my house and let me sleep off a sickness as if I was hung over. "I don't feel well." I tried to smile but it hurt my face.

"Aw, sweetheart, I know you don't." Alec rubbed my forehead. "Do you want your fever to go down naturally or do you want some ibuprofen?"

I shook my head. I hated swallowing pills. I choked one time when I was little and even now I had to crush them up with a spoon and eat them with peanut butter.

A tear escaped my eye and went down my cheek.

"Don't cry, shh, don't cry." Alec gently walked me up the stairs to his room and lay down next to me. His strong arms lifted me into his embrace. "You just have the flu or something. You'll be fine, okay?"

"Promise?" I asked in a tiny voice.

He chuckled and brushed my hair from my face. "I promise. And when you get better I may even let you drive my car."

"Tease." I closed my eyes, liking the way his deep

chuckle sounded with my head against his chest.

"Got some ibuprofen. What the—" Demetri stopped dead in his tracks. My eyes flickered across his face. He looked angry.

"Don't you think her boyfriend should be the one in bed with her, Alec?" Demetri snarled.

"Absolutely." Alec moved away from me. "I'll check back on you in a few." He walked by his brother and said in a low voice, "Try not to make it worse."

"Ass," Demetri mumbled as he slowly approached the bed. For some reason I felt like I was letting him down, like my being sick made him upset with me.

"I'm sorry," I said, choked up again.

He shrugged. "It's okay."

Wait, did he just accept my apology for being sick? What?

"I wish you felt better. I had some plans for you tonight, Nat. Ones that would have put a smile on that gorgeous face of yours."

"I'm sorry," I said again, because I didn't really know what else to say.

He shrugged. "We can't control when we get sick. It's no biggie." He leaned down and kissed my cheek. "I'm gonna let you sleep, okay?"

I nodded, even though I felt a stab of disappointment as I watched him walk out of the room.

Seconds later I heard one of the cars start outside.

What the heck?

"He doesn't like sick people," Alec announced from the doorway.

"Clearly," I mumbled, feeling more and more dejected as the minutes ticked by. My head wasn't pounding near as much. I tried to sit up against the pillows and failed.

"Here." Alec chuckled and stuffed some pillows behind my back.

"So why doesn't he like sick people? Is he a germaphobe

or something?"

"No." Alec sat on the bed with a book in hand. "Our mom left us when we were little, and our dad died of cancer a few years afterwards. Most of Demetri's memories are of the hospital."

"What about yours?"

Alec laughed. "Playing checkers with dad when he didn't feel well enough to walk. Holding his hand when they told him there was nothing else they could do. Reading him books even though I was only ten and probably the worst reader on the planet."

"I like your memories." I sighed.

"Me too." He gave me a smile. "Demetri just deals with things different than most people. It doesn't mean he cares for you any less."

"Why are you always defending him?" The words were out of my mouth before I could stop them. "Forget I said that, please forget I said that." I couldn't escape him, I was trapped in the bed and if I even tried to stand up I was convinced I would collapse on the floor.

"Does it seem that way?" Alec asked looking at me speculatively.

I nodded.

"Hmm, I guess it would. I don't know, Nat, I'm just protective of him. I'm older by a year, it's my job to be protective."

Lame answer, but it was all I was going to get.

"If you're older by a year, and he's a senior and you're a senior."

"Good math, Nat," Alec teased.

"How are you in the same grade?"

"I live to learn," he joked then nudged me.

"High school is like going to hell every day, so why would you willingly choose to go?"

"I never finished. We got busy touring and I kept putting

it off. It's as easy as that. Demetri actually likes learning. He likes studying, even though it doesn't come easy to him. I'd rather do things. I can't sit and listen to someone drone on for hours without wanting to jump out the window."

"And here I thought you liked to sit and contemplate."

He shuddered. "No, it just appears that way."

I yawned.

"You're tired. Go to sleep, Nat."

I shook my head, I knew I was being a baby but I really didn't want to sleep, not if when I woke up he'd be gone too. I hated being alone, which was so silly! I was alone all the time!

"I brought a book." Alec grinned. "I'll be right here, okay?"

"Promise?"

His eyes darkened. "Promise." His whisper lulled me to sleep.

****

"Nat?" Demetri's voice was really close to my head. I opened my eyes and jumped. He was lying on the bed, holding me in his arms. What happened to his phobia of sickness? And where the heck was Alec? He promised.

Defeated, I looked at my boyfriend and managed a small smile.

"These are for you." Demetri reached behind him and pulled out a bouquet of white roses. White, not red. Interesting, and a really good gift, too. Darn him.

"Thanks," I mumbled, and shook my head in hopes that it would clear the sleep and grogginess away.

"I'm sorry I bolted." Demetri sighed "Being sick just freaks me out. Alec said he told you, but it's not really an excuse to leave my girlfriend."

"It's okay."

"No, it's not." Demetri snapped. "Damn, why are you so

easy on me?"

"Fine. It's not okay. I hate you. Take your stupid flowers." I threw them on the floor and crossed my arms.

Demetri grinned. "Much better. What am I going to do with you? Hmm?" His hand blazed a trail down my neck. "You're beautiful, funny… I can't even look at another girl."

"Well, I'm glad the man-whore has finally settled on one girl." Sickness made people braver, I decided.

"Only one." He vowed, then reached down and gently kissed my lips. "Are you really feeling better?"

I thought about it for a second. My head wasn't pounding anymore, though I still felt kinda dizzy even though I was lying down. My legs felt like lead, and my mouth tasted like cotton, but all in all, at least I wasn't as tired as I had been before.

"I think I'm better."

"Hmm…" Demetri threw off my covers, I looked down. Holy crap. Someone undressed me and put me in sweats. Mortified, I closed my eyes.

"Chill, babe. It's not like you're the first girl I've seen naked."

Right. Because that makes me feel better. I grit my teeth and pushed off the bed. "Did you undress me then?"

"It was a team effort."

I wanted to die. "Both you and your brother undressed me? Correct me if I'm wrong, but isn't that sort of thing illegal in all fifty states?"

"Chill, Nat. It's not like we took turns with you or anything."

Without responding, I tried to get up. I needed to get out of there and go home. I was too confused to stay and felt so sick I just wanted to be in my bed. My head was spinning. I put my weight on one foot and then the other, trying to make it to the door. "You can't go around stripping people of their clothes, just because they're sick."

Demetri frowned."But you were uncomfortable. Plus, I'm the one who did it. Alec was here supervising. For some reason he didn't trust me to do the deed without peeking."

"I'm going home," I announced.

"Like hell you are!" Demetri grasped my arm, his fingers digging into my sensitive skin. "You're staying here and that's final. You're sick. You shouldn't be up and walking anyways. Come on." With a grunt he lifted me up and cradled me in his arms. You would think I only weighed ten pounds. He walked briskly down the hall and then down the stairs.

"She try to escape or something?" Alec asked suddenly appearing at the bottom of the stairs. I glared.

Alec put his hands in the air. "She's scary when she's sick."

"She's also suicidal. She wanted to walk home."

Alec scowled. "Nat, you'd make it as far as the kitchen table, pass out, and most likely crack a tooth in the process."

I clenched my teeth to keep form yelling. It wasn't that I wasn't thankful, but I didn't look my best, I didn't feel well, and they were both acting like I was totally unable to take care of myself. Now that my fever was gone I knew I would be fine on my own.

"Lock the doors." Alec's intense gaze met mine. Stupid mind reader.

Demetri put me down on the couch and then walked to the doors, locking each of them. "Crap, how long have they been camped out?"

"Since you came back with the flowers." Alec answered.

"Who's camped out?" I piped up.

"Photographers, news crews, fans. Basically everyone in Oregon." Alec cursed and took a seat next to me. "Thanks to my brother's heroic kiss downtown Seaside, the media can't wait to dig in to you."

"Great," I grumbled at laid my head on the arm of the couch. "If they saw me now they'd wonder what the fuss was all about."

Alec tilted his head. "You really don't see it do you?"

"See what?" I swallowed out of nervousness. Alec's eyes bore into mine as if he was trying to figure out a piece to some giant puzzle. His gaze made me want to squirm, but I was able to keep myself still.

"How breathtaking you are." His eyes shone with appreciation. "Nat, you're absolutely gorgeous without any help from make up or fancy clothes. And you're the only person in the known universe who hasn't asked for one of our autographs."

"She hasn't?" Demetri said walking back into the living room only picking up on the last part of the conversation, "Rude, Nat. Rude."

I laughed. I couldn't help it. "So that's how I get rid of you two? Ask for your autograph and throw my panties like the rest of them?"

Demetri plopped onto the couch in between us. Of course. "I could live without the autograph part, but the panty-throwing sounds intriguing. You planning on doing that soon? I'll wait." He grinned like a little boy. I reached over and kissed his cheek on impulse.

Alec cleared his throat. His eyes moving from me to Demetri then back again. "I'll go see what I can do about the media for now. Why don't you guys watch a movie or something?"

I sighed. "My pick. I'm sick."

Demetri cursed. "My head hurts, does that count?"

"Your head always hurts when you use it, silly, so no, doesn't count," I joked.

Alec left the room laughing, while Demetri scowled playfully.

Chapter Thirteen

We watched movies until the wee hours of the night. By midnight I felt loads better, which was good considering I'd have to sneak back into my house.

Demetri had fallen asleep so it was up to Alec to deliver me to the front door in one piece.

"Ready?" he whispered as he unlocked the back door.

I nodded.

We padded across the backyard and quickly made it to my back door. Everything was dark, meaning the photographers had finally gone home.

"Everything's going go to change, Nat," Alec whispered behind me. I turned, his eyes looked black in the darkness, not the usual green I had grown so accustomed to.

"What do you mean?" My voice didn't hide my panic.

"You're going to be on every news station, every radio station, every gossip site. I just want you to know, it's about to change and it's not going to be easy."

"They'll get bored with me," I reassured him by reaching up for a hug. His arms were so big and strong. I shivered when he placed his chin on my head.

"Nobody could ever get bored with you, Nat. That's impossible."

I smiled. "You're just being nice because I'm sick."

His chuckle warmed me. He pulled back and looked into my eyes. "I'm not just being nice, I'm being honest. Now get some rest." Alec's head descended, his lips were almost to my cheek when a flash interrupted us.

"Get in the house, Nat. Now." Alec frantically pushed me into the house and walked up to the photographers. He was yelling. Wow, I must bring out the hulk in him. He always seems so calm and collected. Right now it looks like he's going to rip the guy's head off.

The guy started cussing him out. Alec raised his arms above his head again. Oh no, this is not good.

I quickly dialed Demetri's number. It went to voicemail. I called five more times before he finally answered.

His voice was groggy. "This better be a booty call."

I ignored him. "There are photographers outside. Alec is yelling at them. He looks crazy. I don't know what to do."

Demetri cursed and the line went dead.

I watched as he ran out of the house in nothing but his low slung jeans. His tan body glowed in the moonlight. He was every inch as beautiful as Alec, but so different. Alec was covered in tattoos. Demetri had two, though I couldn't make it out. It too spread across his chest and seemed to connect to something on his back. It was too hard to tell in the dark, but I could have sworn there was writing.

Demetri grabbed Alec and ushered him back into the house, while Alec was still yelling.

The photographer walked away in the other direction. I locked my door just in case and walked up to my room. Cell phone clenched in my hand. What the heck was that about? He took a picture? So what? Not that I didn't appreciate Alec's protectiveness, but still.

I checked my phone again. No texts from Demetri. I put

my cell by my pillow anyway and drifted off to sleep.

Chapter Fourteen

My entire Sunday was dedicated to homework. Demetri had his fair share as well, so we agreed to hang out Monday at school. I didn't just miss him, I missed Alec too. But I knew it would be weird to just stop by their house. After all, I basically stayed the weekend with them.

My mom didn't even ask how I was when she walked in Sunday night. She scurried into her office and said she had an emergency client. Which basically meant there was some sort of suicide attempt.

I shrugged.

My mind still itched to know why Alec and Demetri were seeing my mom. It wasn't as if I could ask her what they talked with her about. And neither of them would say a word to me about it.

It just seemed like there was so much more to the story. Why were they really here? The situation bothered me more than it should because I was stuck smack dab in the middle of it. And yes, I guess I am semi-insecure, I just didn't want to be caught up in something that would eventually hurt me.

The next day I accidently overslept. I only had time to

brush my teeth, wash my face, and throw on clothes before I was running out the door to my truck.

Only, it was missing. I blinked several times. Maybe I was losing my mind? Who the heck would steal my truck?

"Geez, took you long enough to get ready," Demetri said from behind me. I flipped around and felt myself blush.

"I overslept."

"I couldn't tell." He eyed me appreciatively making my blush burn my cheeks like crazy.

"Do it again," he whispered as he leaned in and kissed me.

"What?"

"Blush. It's sexy." His arms came around me lifting me off the ground. I giggled as he twirled me around then set me down. "You ready, man?" He called behind him.

Alec bounded out of the house. He was wearing some sort of graphic T-shirt and skinny jeans with Converse. I never liked skinny jeans on guys. I liked them on him. A lot.

I blushed again, but this time I turned away from Demetri. It wouldn't go over well if I was caught blushing because of his brother.

"Let's go." Alec got into his car an unlocked the doors. The drive to school felt tense. I had no idea why but all I kept thinking was that I was somehow the reason for it. I looked between both guys and saw that neither of them looked happy.

Demetri's cell phone ring jolted me enough to make me almost smack my head against the window.

"I'm sorry, what?" he roared. "How the hell did that happen?"

Lots of cursing followed and then he threw the phone to the floor of the car.

"How bad?" Alec asked quietly.

"Bad."

"Atlanta bad?"

"Worse, man, so much worse." Demetri turned around and bit his lip. "I don't know how to say this, or even how to warn you."

"Just say it," Alec spat.

Demetri gave his brother a glare before reaching for my hand and kissing it. "The media's cooked up a pretty ridiculous story. It's not going to be an easy day."

"What kind of story?"

My eyes flickered between the two of them. Alec's hands were gripping the steering wheel so hard it looked like he was going to break it off.

Demetri cleared his throat. "One where you were seen kissing one brother one night, only to be seen almost kissing the other the next night."

"So they labeled me a whore?"

Alec slammed on the breaks and put the car into park smack dab in the middle of the road. Luckily it was Seaside, so no traffic.

His eyes were furious. "Don't you dare ever call yourself that. Do you understand?"

I nodded, suddenly scared. I hadn't ever seen him this mad.

Demetri put his hand on Alec's arm. He looked like a man possessed. I could see every muscle tense in his body. Finally, he turned back and we were on our way to school again.

"So what's the plan?"

Demetri looked shocked. "How are you not more upset?"

I shrugged. "I missed breakfast and didn't have my morning coffee. I have no energy to be upset."

Alec cursed again and reached into the glove box pulling out a protein bar. "You gotta eat, Nat. You were sick this weekend."

It was on the tip of my tongue to say, *Thanks, Mom,* but something told me he wasn't in the joking mood.

I nibbled on the bar as Demetri talked. "You're my girlfriend, people know that. We'll just have to do some damage control. And don't be seen alone with Alec."

"That won't be a problem." Alec put the car in park, turned off the ignition and jumped out.

"He feels responsible." Demetri sighed. "He's not mad at you."

I nodded, tears suddenly clogging my throat.

"Nat, look at me." I did.

Demetri placed his hands on either side of my face. "You have to be brave, okay?"

"Okay." I bit my lip. "I can do that."

"That's my girl." Demetri hopped out of the car and opened my door.

We walked hand in hand into the school amidst the awkward stares and whispers as we made our way down the hall.

Some students took pictures, others pointed and laughed. I wanted to die a thousand deaths. Within minutes a few giant men greeted me at my locker. They weren't high schoolers, not unless we were suddenly putting steroids in the baseball team's hot lunch.

One had a tattoo that covered most of his head. His neck was the size of my thigh, and I immediately decided that if I wanted someone killed, this is the dude I would hire for the job.

The other was a little shorter but by no means smaller. If anything his size was more intimidating. His arms protruded from his body as if his muscles were too big to be kept down. His eyes were a steely gray. A black goatee lined his mouth and chin.

They were both in jeans and black T-shirts.

"Security?" I asked, lamely hoping my voice didn't sound as freaked out as I really was.

They both gave curt nods.

Demetri was busy texting. I nudged him.

"Sorry, guys, didn't see you."

Didn't see them? NASA could see them! I rolled my eyes in annoyance as Demetri finally put his phone away and gave us his full attention.

"Bob." He motioned to the guy with the tattoo on his head. Somehow the name Bob seemed out of place, call me crazy. "You're going to shadow Nat for the remainder of the school year."

The man nodded.

I felt sick.

"Why am I getting shadowed?" I pleaded.

"Because." Demetri reached into his back pocket revealing his phone. He flipped through something then held it out to me. I took it in my hands and gasped nearly dropping the thing onto the ground.

The headline read, "Local Girl Bags AD2!"

My hands shook as I scrolled through the incriminating photos. The first one was of me and Demetri holding hands at dinner and kissing outside. It didn't look so bad, but paired with the picture of Alec on my doorstep leaning in toward my face…

I really did look like a whore.

How they were able to make that picture look like more than it was, irritated and hurt me. Is this why Alec was so mad?

With fury I slammed the phone back into Demetri's hand. He sighed. "Nat, it's going to be fine. Even if it means I need to run through the streets screaming and drunk so they don't focus on you."

"Wouldn't you do that normally?" I asked, not sure why I was joking with him after seeing my whole life crumble before me.

"Hilarious." Demetri rolled his eyes. "Now, Bob has been instructed to keep tabs on you all day, especially when I can't, oh and here…" He pulled out a sleek iPhone 5. "You'll need this."

"I have a phone."

"You have a dinosaur. Take the phone, Nat."

"Since when are PDA's dinosaurs?"

"I thought you had computers here?" Demetri looked genuinely confused. "People don't use crap PDAs anymore, not when they can have an iPhone. Don't be mad, but I programmed some numbers in there in case of emergencies. You'll have to add the ones you need too, and you'll also have to text the friends you trust and give them your new number."

I took the phone and nodded. It felt heavy in my hand as if I was taking some sort of bribe money from someone. But I knew they were just doing this to protect me.

I walked to class. Nobody talked to me. Crap, they didn't even look at me. I blamed Bob.

I told him so, too.

He smiled, which actually gave me hope that he wouldn't kill me when the brothers weren't watching.

By the time the lunch bell rang, I was ready to scream. I walked into the bathroom. A girl nudged me and mumbled *bitch* under her breath. Naturally, Bob went into the bathroom with me, which helped considering he glared at the girl and gave me a look that said, "I'll kill her if you want. Just say the word." I shook my head, and once the bathroom was "clear," whatever that meant, I was able to be left in peace. Great, as if high school wasn't bad enough, now security had to check the stalls for crazy people.

I stood in line for a salad.

"So, life sucks?" Evan said next to me.

I shook my head. "Only today."

"I'm sorry, Nat. If it makes you feel better. I don't believe everything I see on TV, and even if I did, I'm most likely the type that would give you a fist pump or high five for managing to bag two of the biggest rock stars on the planet."

"Thanks," I mumbled. "I think."

"It was a compliment." Evan laughed and reached for an apple. "So, how long until you decide to homeschool?"

"Not funny." I nudged him and pushed my tray forward. The lunch lady gave me a tiny bit of salad, enough to feed a small bunny, and put a carrot on top.

"Yum," Evan whispered next to me.

I giggled again. I had forgotten how much Evan was able to cheer me up when I was feeling slightly emotional and irrational.

"How goes Hell day?" Demetri asked behind me.

Evan answered for me. "A girl called her a bitch behind her back, another called her a whore, and I could have sworn someone just pushed her."

"Thanks, Evan." I saluted him and rolled my eyes.

"He's being dramatic."

Evan lifted his eyebrows. "Me, dramatic?"

"See?" I pointed at him and gave Demetri a reassuring smile.

He didn't smile back. If anything his scowl ran deeper. "Who do they think they are? They can't treat you like that! You're my girlfriend!"

"Yeah, I don't think they really care." I picked up my tray, balancing it with my water bottle. "And to answer your question, they're high schoolers. Imagine Hollywood only the drugs are cheaper, the women are looser, the men are hornier, and everyone's hormones are spiked like they're high on ecstasy."

"Wow, Nat," Evan said behind me. "That was actually quite accurate. I'm impressed."

I nodded my head.

Demetri still wasn't smiling. "What can I do?"

"Other than threatening everyone in school?" I lifted my eyebrows. "Let it blow over. They'll have to give up after a while."

Bob followed me to the table. The other security guy, whose name I discovered was Lloyd, stood near the drinking fountain.

My eyes scanned the room until they landed on Alec.

He was smiling.

What the heck? Wasn't he still pissed about this morning?

The girl sitting next to him was touching his arm. Jealousy was not something I was familiar with, but ever since meeting Alec, I was filled with it. And then I felt guilty because in that same instant, Demetri sat next to me and wrapped his arm around me forcing me into a hug. "I'm so sorry for all this, Babe."

I pulled away and gave him a tight smile. "It's fine."

My breathing was labored as I looked down at my food then peeked through my hair back at Alec. He was still smiling. The girl was still touching.

I willed him to look at me.

When our eyes met I continued to glare.

His smile disappeared. He whispered in the girl's ear and walked off, leaving her pouting alone at the table.

A surge of guilt washed over me as I drank some water and watched him exit the cafeteria completely. "I, uh… I'll be right back. Need to use the restroom."

I pried myself from Demetri's grasp and ran out into the hall.

My eyes darted from left to right. Where did he go?

And then a hand came from behind and covered my mouth, pulling me into the janitor's closet.

"Don't scream, it's just me." Alec's warm breath was on my neck. He released me and gently turned me to face him. I had the strongest urge to jump into his arms and cry.

"What was that about, Nat?"

"What do you mean?" I played dumb.

"Don't play dumb," he said, as if reading my thoughts again.

Biting my lip, I sighed.

"Don't do that anymore, please." His voice was rough and low. Chills wracked my body.

"Do what?"

"Bite your lip, it's distracting as hell."

"Okay." I almost did it again but licked my lips instead.

He laughed. "Yeah, like that's better." He pushed me a little so we had more space between us and sighed. "Now, are you going to tell me why you were trying to kill me with your mind in the cafeteria?"

Embarrassment washed over me, I looked down at my feet. "You were smiling."

Silence.

"And," I continued. "It wasn't at me."

Alec exhaled.

"I know it's stupid. I know how ridiculous I sound, but you were so angry this morning in the car and you never smile at me at school, and now it's even worse because you said you're going to try to stay away from me, and I really don't want you to. I want you to be… close."

"You talk a lot when you're nervous."

"A habit I'm trying to break," I retorted.

"Nat…" His hands moved to my shoulders. I closed my eyes as the feeling of completeness washed over me. "We both know I can't be close to you."

"They're just pictures," I grumbled.

"It's not about the pictures."

My head snapped up. His eyes were hooded, his lips parted just slightly as his mouth hovered near mine.

Chapter Fifteen

My body screamed *kiss me*! But that would be wrong, and cheating, and it would prove exactly what the papers had written about me.

I told myself to step back but I was caught, hypnotized by his eyes, his mouth, everything about him.

"Nat…" He groaned. He looked so tortured.

I reached up and touched his face. Alec closed his eyes, muttering a curse under his breath.

"We can't."

"Can't?" I swallowed the lump in my throat.

"Us, we can never happen, Nat."

I jerked back. "Why?"

"I promised someone a long time ago that I would never get in the way again. He really likes you, Nat. Possibly loves you. I won't do that to him. I can't do that to him, regardless of how I feel about you."

"How do you feel?" I felt my eyes search his face for any hint of information that would give him away.

"Guilty." He growled as his mouth crushed mine. I closed my eyes as his lips worked against mine. Alec was so different. His kiss didn't scare me — it terrified me. It made me feel things a high school girl had no right to feel.

Alec stumbled back, his breathing ragged. "Goodbye, Nat."

Hurt, I watched him leave the janitor's closet. He didn't come back, even though I waited.

After ten minutes the lunch bell rang and I walked to my locker in a daze of confusion.

"Hey." Demetri caught up to me. "You sick again?"

"No, sorry. I'm just tired," I lied, hoping my face didn't say *"And I just kissed your brother, because I think I may love him."*

The problem was I loved Demetri too. In a totally different but very real way, and I felt so guilty that I had just done something so horrible to him.

"You need coffee." He nodded his head as if he was the all-knowing and all powerful Oz and I the Tin Man who was just given a heart.

"Yes, I do."

"Come on." He held out his hand. I grabbed it. Demetri led me through the crowded halls, the security detail followed close behind.

When we got to the principal's office, it was clear that any woman with a heartbeat would gladly murder me and take my place. For one second I thought the receptionist was going to rip her own shirt off and confess undying love.

I quickly grabbed her family picture and put it face down on the counter while Demetri smooth talked her. Nobody should have to witness this tragedy.

After a few minutes, in which I watched him sign a few autographs for the office staff, he winked at me and we were off.

"Did you just use bribery?"

"No." He laughed. "I smiled."

I chuckled. "What am I going to do with you? So cocky…"

"Anything you want, Nat. I'm yours." He stopped walking and pulled me into his embrace. His lips were on mine before I could protest.

Guiltily, I kissed him harder. I wanted the memory of Alec's lips gone. I was still hurt, and now I was using Demetri to make me feel better. He moaned and wrapped his arms around me, crushing my body against his. Muscles flexed in his jaw as I leaned up and kissed his chin.

"Nat," he ground out tearing himself away from me. "If you keep kissing me back like that, I'm not going to behave."

I bit my lip, then quickly remembered Alec's earlier warning. As if I summoned him up out of nowhere, he walked up behind us, his lips in a grim line.

"Skipping school?"

"Nat wasn't feeling well." Demetri shrugged.

"I wonder why. She looked fine in your arms a few seconds ago." His eyes were accusing.

I wanted to scream, *So what? Yes, I kissed my boyfriend, and yes, it was minutes after kissing you! But you said no! You practically threw me into your brother's arms, and now you think you have a right to be mad at me?*

I felt my nostrils flare. Alec took a step back, then smirked. "Whatever, I just came outside to grab something from the car. You kids have fun." And just like that he was gone.

And my heart was in my throat for the second time that day.

"Come on." Demetri unlocked the car.

"How's Alec going to get home?" I buckled my seatbelt and watched his disappearing form as he reentered the school.

"I left Lloyd with him, he'll catch a ride. Don't worry, my brother is very capable of taking care of himself."

"Right." I knew that. I just didn't need Demetri to know that I knew that.

"So…" Demetri turned the key in the ignition and put the

car in reverse. "I have all afternoon and then I need to go to your mom's for an appointment."

"Do you guys go every week?" I pried, fidgeting with my hair.

"Yup." His expression was so horribly closed.

"You and Alec."

Silence and then, "Of course."

I rolled my eyes. "When are you going to trust me?" The car stopped at the stop sign leading out into traffic.

"When I know I can." This time his eyes never left my face as he looked intently into my eyes. I felt so small, I wanted to crawl underneath the car and let it roll over me. Did he know about me and Alec? Was I that obvious?

Demetri cursed and pulled the car over on the side of the road. "Wanna tell me right here and right now so we can get this over with?"

"What do you mean?"

Demetri laughed and looked out the window. "I think you know exactly what I mean."

I pretended to be clueless even though my breathing was ragged and I was suddenly hot all over.

Demetri cursed. "My brother is off limits. I don't share."

"And I do?" I blurted. "What about the cheerleader you were making out with at the party?"

Demetri hit the steering wheel and cursed. "I thought you were over that! It was a mistake! Alright? Besides this is different."

"It's different how? You want me to trust you? Then you have to trust me!" Even as I said it I felt like crap, but I hated that he was making me feel guilty over something he was doing just a few weeks ago.

"He's my brother, Nat. There are things you don't know. It wouldn't be the first time a girl had the hots for both of us and went for it, okay?"

"I'm not that kind of girl."

"You sure?" he snapped.

"That was uncalled for." Hands shaking, I opened the door to the car, climbed out, and began walking up the street in the opposite direction.

"Nat, stop!" Demetri ran after me and pulled me into his arms. "I'm sorry, I just get so damned jealous. I see the way he looks at you. The way you look at him."

"It's not like that," I lied. "It won't ever be like that. Believe me, he's made it very clear where his loyalty lies." And it wasn't with me or with his feelings for me, but for his brother who was doing everything in his power to prove to me that he was worthy, while I went behind his back. I was the worst of the worst, and I knew I had to make a choice. I couldn't have feelings for Alec and date Demetri. I needed to let one of them go.

"But have you made your intentions known? Have you made your choice, Nat?" Demetri asked his lips a breath away from mine. "Because up until now, I've had my doubts."

My mind replayed the images of Alec's laughter, of our stolen moments together. The way his kiss felt against my lips. And then the sound of his goodbye. I sighed and licked my lips. *Goodbye Alec*. "I want you."

Demetri's stoic face suddenly broke out into the widest grin I'd ever seen. "You mean it?" He kissed my lips. "Tell me you mean it." His hands were in my hair, threading it between his fingers.

"I mean it." And I did. Because part of me loved him, part of me craved him. But another part would always belong to Alec. I just chose in that moment to tuck it away. Maybe if I ignored it, I wouldn't feel the sting of rejection anymore. Maybe I could move on and actually be happy with Demetri.

"I really care about you, Nat. I've never felt this way before," he whispered across my lips. His tongue licked my lower lip, and then he tugged it with his teeth as his mouth covered mine again.

"Me either," I admitted, because I hadn't ever felt this way before. I just didn't expect to feel it twice.

A few cars honked in the distance. I felt myself blush as I noticed we were only a mile away from school and making out in the street. With our luck it would probably hit the news tonight. Great. That's all I needed. My mom to suspect I was not only sleeping with both boys but skipping school with them too.

I groaned and slapped my palm against my forehead. All this drama was exhausting.

Demetri chuckled and reached around me, tugging my body in for a quick hug. "Food?"

"Food." I nodded.

Chapter Sixteen

The next few weeks fell into a very nice and familiar rhythm. Demetri and Alec always took me to school and Bob followed me like a stalker every day. I even convinced him it would be in his best interest to join me at work.

He liked that.

He was currently on flavor thirty of five thousand flavors of taffy.

It never ceased to crack me up to see him digging through the different flavors and tasting them.

Even Evan warmed up to him. Well as much as you can to a guy who grunts more than he talks.

I didn't see Alec. Ever. I still ran with him, but when we ran it was exactly as it had been before. We didn't talk about anything personal and the miles always ended before I was ready for them be done.

At school he ignored me completely. Because of that fact, everyone forgot about my whorish newspaper spread and began talking about Homecoming and the upcoming football game.

I was happy.

I still missed Alec, but Demetri had been the best boyfriend a girl could ask for. He was attentive, charismatic, and caring. Sometimes, his ego got on my nerves, but I was comfortable enough with him to tell him when he was being a selfish pig.

Although his response was always confusion. Which always meant I had to explain to him why it didn't sound good for him to refer to himself in the third person, or talk about a new car he wanted to buy in front of a girl who was using food stamps at the grocery store.

I was finally able to focus on something other than boys when my teachers decided our finals before the end of the first quarter would last three days and consist of nothing but papers and tests.

Who still did finals every quarter?

I was on my third and final test and ready to freak out when Demetri came strolling down the hall with Starbucks in hand.

"For me?" I asked, breathless.

He held out the coffee then snatched it away.

"I'm going to hurt you," I spat.

"So violent." Demetri sat next to me in the hall. I was doing a last minute cram session before the next test started.

"So tired," I grumbled, leaning my head on his shoulder.

"The coffee is because you're tired." He held it out, but attached to the back of the cup was an envelope. I snatched it and opened it up.

It was a poem.

"You wrote me a poem?"

"No." He shook his head as if disgusted. "I wrote you a song."

Oh. My. Gosh.

"Y-you did?" I didn't know what to say.

"Yup, I'm recording it with Alec when we have time."

"Wait, I thought you wrote it though?"

Demetri leaned in and kissed me lightly across the mouth. "I did, though he always helps with some of the verses, plus we always sing together."

If I wouldn't have already been sitting I probably would have fainted. The words hit too close to home. It was too real. And suddenly I felt like crying.

"Hey, hey! Why are you crying?" Demetri chuckled and pulled me into his chest. "Baby, I thought it would make you happy!"

"It does, I mean, I am. I guess I'm just touched. Nobody's ever done anything like this for me."

"You deserve everything." He kissed my nose. If only he knew what I liar I was. I exhaled.

"About Homecoming…"

My head popped up. He had all my attention. "Yeah?"

"I have this thing in L.A. It's a music camp. A lot of the low income schools participate, and it lasts for a week. I offered to help teach some classes, and well, they called yesterday. I leave tonight." His eyes were sad but more excited than I've seen them in a while.

"You need to go," I said, happily squeezing his hand.

"You don't mind?" He grinned. "Because, Nat, I can totally cancel, I mean… Well, I would be bummed. I found out I really like teaching, and I'm good at it, and I don't know. It's just so different than performing all the time, and—"

He had the same issue I did with talking. Whenever he got excited it was impossible to shut him up. I pulled him into a hug and laughed even though a stab of disappointment was barreling into my chest. Maybe it was for the best since I hadn't bought a dress yet. Demetri had said we could make a huge date out of dress shopping. Guess that was out the window too. I pushed back from the hug and sighed. "Demetri, just go! I'm proud of you and I'll be fine. I'll just go with Alesha and Evan."

Demetri groaned.

"What?"

"Evan's gonna be pissed."

"Evan will deal with it." I nudged him. "Plus, it's nothing you can't fix with free concert tickets."

"Aw, there's my little manipulator." He got up and dusted his jeans off.

My eyes followed his hands as he shoved them into his pocket. I didn't want to admit that I was worried about him going to L.A. without Big Brother watching over him. My doubts were unfounded though. I mean, he'd been doing nothing but proving to me he was trustworthy. "I promise I'll call you when I can, okay? I'm flying out of Portland in a few hours, so I'll let you drink your awesome coffee and read the amazing song I wrote you." He looked like he was going to say something and cleared his throat. "I, um, I'll miss you, Nat."

My heart nearly broke. He was so good. I didn't deserve him. "I'll miss you too, Demetri." I got up and kissed him. "Now go pack, and try to behave when you're away."

"Scout's honor."

"You were never a Boy Scout."

"I would have been an awesome Boy Scout," he argued.

"Just go." I pushed him down the hall and joined him in laughter as he waved goodbye.

I walked back to my seat and glanced at the song Demetri had written.

Brown eyes, blond hair, I can't help but stare. She's got me hypnotized. I need her, like oxygen, I can't explain the way she makes me feel inside. Like rain, washing my fears away, she makes me feel like I can say all those things I'm too scared to say.

Breathe in, breathe out, sometimes you just gotta shout your love. Shout your love. Inhale, exhale, the beauty of your love will always be enough. Enough.

Lost, the feeling I have without you. Like I can't function and don't know what to do. It's like I'm dreaming while I'm waking. Like

I'm suffocating. Being with her is my addiction, and I don't want to have to stop. No, I never want to stop. Like rain, washing my fears away, she makes me feel like I can say all those things I'm too scared to say.

Come back to me. Come back to me. I swear I won't ever leave. I don't think I have it in me. I can't fight, I can't fight. If I did, I would lose, if only it meant I could have you. Cause I need you.

Like rain.

Like rain.

Like rain, washing my fears away.

I stared at the song. Tears welled in my eyes. I knew exactly the part that Alec had written. It was the bridge. I could almost hear his voice singing it.

I quickly texted Demetri and said thank you.

A smiley face was his reply.

Carefully, I folded the song and put it in my pocket then trudged to class. It was my last final before the long weekend and the Homecoming game.

The coffee helped me get through the first hour.

By two I still had a few questions left.

Whoever said that school wasn't torture was clearly homeschooled, or didn't attend public high school.

"Ugh," I moaned, then realized it was out loud. Evan snickered behind me. I was surprised he was still there, all things considering. His tactic during tests usually had to do with him filling in the circles in as many designs as possible.

"Five minutes," Mr. Meservy announced.

I looked behind me. Alec was hovering over his paper like it was life or death. I quickly filled in the last few circles, because I was clueless about the answers, and brought my test to the front.

"Thank you." Mr. Meservy took my test.

Done. I was done!

I ran out into the hall and had the ridiculous notion to throw my fist in the air and start belting Zac Efron from High

School Musical. Clearly, I was losing my mind. Demetri would be so disappointed. Both he and Alec had been dead set against me listening to anyone that they deemed threatening in the music world.

Goodbye, Neo, both Justins, Drake, Hunter Hayes — so basically, they just disapproved of the males.

I did a little dance in the hall anyway.

"Is that from High School Musical?" A familiar voice said behind me.

I froze, my hand mid-air as if I was doing the clock move, and turned. Alec's grin was so wide it looked like it hurt his face.

He also had his phone out.

"Please tell me you didn't take a picture."

"I didn't take a picture," he confirmed.

I exhaled.

"I recorded it and just uploaded to Youtube."

"No!" I gasped.

"Nah." Alec shrugged. "But I did send it to Demetri."

I glowered at him as he chuckled and put his phone in his pocket. This was the most we had talked in weeks. I tried to extinguish the memory of his lips on mine, but it was pointless.

I exhaled and put my hands on my hips. "What do you want?"

"Don't ask a question you don't want the answer to," he said darkly.

"Sorry."

He shrugged. "Demetri wants me to take you to Homecoming."

"Demetri is very trusting." I glanced at Alec's reaction to my comment, but he feigned indifference.

"Demetri knows where my loyalty lies."

"So do I."

We stood there glaring at one another for what seemed

like hours.

"Look..." Alec cursed and walked toward me. He always scratched the back of his head when he was nervous, and I always stared as his shirt barely rose, giving me a small glimpse of his stomach and part of his tattoo. "We're friends. Let me take you. It would suck to go by yourself."

"True." I folded my arms across my chest. "I just don't know if it's the best idea."

"I'll be the perfect gentleman."

That's what I'm afraid of. I mean, crap. What am I thinking? I love Demetri, I love him! He's been so good to me, and he wrote that song, and... Ugh. I nodded at Alec. "I'll go with you. Thank you for asking."

He beamed.

My heart felt confused. After a few more moments of awkward stilted conversation we parted ways.

I ran to my truck and hopped in. I needed a dress and fast.

Where to find a dress in Seaside?

I knew Demetri had probably forgotten about our little deal to go together today. He was too excited about teaching. I needed to stop feeling sorry for myself. I quickly said goodbye to Bob and promised him I'd keep my cell phone around. Geez, the guy was nearly impossible to get rid of at school, but the minute I said *dress shopping* he backed off. Men.

I decided to drive the hour and half to Lincoln City. They had more choices and I needed more choices.

The drive took longer than it should have. Traffic was always awful on Highway 101, and I knew first hand that when tourists were pouring into town what should take an hour could take upward of three.

Chapter Seventeen

After almost two hours of traffic, I pulled into Daisy's, a classic dress shop that I knew would have exactly what I needed. I only had a few hours before I was due back home. Not that my parents would even notice if I was gone, but still I was a rule follower.

The bell chimed as I stepped in. Colors and sparkles bombarded my senses until I felt slightly dizzy. I walked up to the plainest dress I could find and looked at the ticket. One hundred and twenty dollars. Not too bad, I guess.

I touched one of the fabrics. It was a dark red. It had a plunging neckline and was floor length.

"You don't want that one," a girl said.

I looked up. She was standing behind the counter filing her nails. Her hair was a dark brown and piled up on top of her head with a pencil sticking in it. "Trust me." She shook her head. "The last girl who bought that dress is so not gonna get any action tonight."

"Good." I felt relieved. "Action is the last thing I want."

The shop girl peered at me. "Really? Because you're really pretty, I mean, I'm not hitting on you or anything, but you have like amazing eyelashes."

I laughed. *So I've been told*. "Thanks."

"Don't get me wrong, but red wouldn't look that great on you. I mean, it would be fine, but I'm thinking silver."

"Silver?" I asked.

She nodded and walked around the counter. "I have the perfect one."

Well, it wasn't as if I was super fashion forward. Alec would probably want me to look nice, and Demetri would like the pictures. I found myself following her through the store, a ghost of a smile on my lips.

"This would be perfect!" My eyes fell to the short cocktail dress in her hands. It was strapless but had some sort of dip in the middle.

"What's that called?" I pointed at the top of the dress where it seemed to curve towards the chest.

She looked at me like I was high. "That's a sweetheart neckline. Haven't you ever worn a cocktail dress before?"

"That would be a no." I awkwardly stuffed my hands in my jean pockets.

"Well, The sweetheart should look killer on you, plus you've got long legs and this baby will make 'em look even longer. Here, try it on." She shoved the dress at me. "I guessed you at about a four or six, is that right?"

"I think so?" I wasn't actually sure. I've never owned a dress like this before.

"Okay, well let me know if you need help." She walked back to the register.

I took a deep breath and stepped behind the curtain. The dress was really smooth and frail. The silver was shimmery and stopped right at the hip where it flared out. It looked like something a fairy princess would wear.

I laughed and began stripping.

Nervously, I looked at the finished product in the mirror.

"You done?" the girl yelled.

"Um, yeah, just a second." I took off my socks, because the dress looked weird with them, and stepped out.

"No. Way!" She clapped her hands. "You look like a super model."

"Really?" I exhaled and turned around to look in the mirror. "You don't think it's too much?"

I had a bit of cleavage and she was right my legs looked dangerously long. I felt awkward and tall, but pretty at the same time.

"Yes. It's too much, but it's perfect. You have shoes?"

And like that she was off.

By the time I drove home an hour later. I had earrings, shoes, a bracelet, and a two hundred dollar dress. At least I knew my parents wouldn't care. They probably wouldn't even notice the hit on the credit card.

My cell rang the minute I drove out of the parking lot, but because of Oregon laws I couldn't actually talk on it without getting a ticket. I hit speakerphone without looking at it and answered.

"Hello?"

"Nat! How are you?" Demetri gushed.

"Good! You on the plane yet?"

"Yeah, we're getting ready to taxi. I just wanted to call and make sure you weren't mad at me."

"Mad?" I repeated.

"You know, for making Alec take you to Homecoming. I just didn't want you to go by yourself."

"I'm not mad." I smiled and shook my head. "And thanks, it was very sweet of you."

"I'm a sweet guy."

"Yes, you are," I confirmed, laughing.

"I gotta run, Nat. I, um. I…" He paused, the only thing I could hear was his breathing on the other end. "I'll miss you."

"I'll miss you too," I whispered.

The call ended and I was filled with so much self-loathing

that I wanted to pull over and cry. He was such a good guy! Why did I have to have such a strong connection with Alec too? It wasn't fair.

Driving home proved tedious when the rain started coming down in sheets. Exhausted, I almost forgot to turn off the lights to my truck when I slammed my door and began running to the house.

With a curse I ran back to the truck and reached inside. I looked up and glimpsed the brothers' house. Alec was watching me.

Shirtless.

I gulped, my hand slid against the switch, and rain pelted my legs. Finally, the lights turned off, I slammed the door and ran into the house tucking the dress bag as far under me as I could.

Rain dripped off my clothes as I stomped up the stairs, a little irritated that my mom still hadn't come out of her cocoon of an office to say hi and congratulate me for making it home in the rain and not dying. By the time I made it to the top of the staircase I heard my mom's office door click open.

"You home, Honey?"

"Yup," I called.

"Okay." The door clicked shut again.

Not another sound from downstairs. Figures. Once in my room, I walked over to the bathroom and turned the shower on.

With a sigh I turned back around. "Holy crap, what are you doing here?"

Alec stood, still shirtless, his eyes menacing, and arms crossed on his chest. "What am I doing here?" He ran his hand through his hair.

"In my room," I clarified. *Shirtless.*

"Do you realize how worried I've been about you?"

"Worried?" My heart lurched. Nobody worried about me. "Why?"

"You disappeared, Nat! When I came back to the house your truck was gone. You weren't at work, you weren't downtown… I waited for hours!"

"I don't understand?"

"Haven't you seen the weather report?"

Dumbly, I shook my head no.

"A huge storm is coming in tonight, they're telling people to stay inside, and here you are driving around as if the damn sun is shining!"

I gulped. "I'm sorry. I didn't know."

"Where'd you go?" he demanded as he paced in front of me.

I looked away and shook my head. "Not that it's any of your business, but Lincoln City."

Alec cursed and turned away from me, stretching his arms behind his head like he wanted to hit something but thought better of it. He whipped back around. "Listen, Nat. I'm only nineteen. It's not good for my health to be thinking about all the awful things that could happen to you in the rain."

"It's just rain."

He looked disgusted. "No, it's not. Things happen, you can lose control, your car can slip, people die." His eyes suddenly broke away from mine and I knew.

"Was it raining when—"

"Yes." His voice was hoarse.

"I'm sorry."

"You should be."

Irritation pumped through me. I approached him, hands on my hips. "I was getting a dress."

Confusion filled his eyes and then realization. He looked down. "For Homecoming."

"Yes."

"May I see it?"

"No."

Alec scowled. "Next time, will you just tell me where you're going? So I don't have a heart attack before twenty?"

I sighed. "Yes, but why didn't you just text me?"

"I think your phone died."

I pursed my lips, then walked over to my purse and pulled out my phone. Sure enough, it was dead. Must have been on low battery when I talked to Demetri. I plugged the charger into it and turned back around to face Alec. "Satisfied?"

A smile played at his lips. "Sure."

"Put on a shirt or something, you're making me nervous, and I'm already edgy enough what with having to drive two hours through the rain."

"Sorry," he mumbled then looked around the room, clearly he wasn't thinking about anything but shimmying up to my window and punishing me for being irresponsible.

I rolled my eyes. "Here." I still had one of his old shirts that I had washed after I was sick.

He turned around to put on the shirt. I have no idea why. Boys. But as he turned I caught a glimpse of his tattoo. It truly mirrored his brother's.

"Hey."

He paused mid-air.

"Doesn't Demetri have that same tattoo?"

Alec continued putting the shirt on and turned to face me. "Yup. You should take a shower, Nat. Warm up a bit."

"And what are you going to do?"

He shrugged. "Make you dinner."

"My mom will freak if she sees you downstairs."

"Nat, your mom won't even know I'm here."

I still wasn't convinced.

"Nat. Shower. Now."

I rolled my eyes and stomped into the bathroom.

The warm water felt heavenly against my skin. I didn't realize how cold I was until I kept turning the shower hotter and hotter.

After twenty minutes, I realized if I didn't actually get out of the shower then Alec would knock the door down.

I wrapped the towel around me and walked out of the bathroom.

Alec was sitting on my bed, a tray of food next to him and a few cans of soda.

I gasped. Didn't he ever knock? What? Was he going to help me dress too?

His gaze met mine and immediately I turned away. I know what I saw in that gaze. His eyes reflected mine and it wasn't right. It wasn't fair.

"Sorry, I thought you brought your clothes into the bathroom."

"Nope." I turned back around and stared him down.

He grinned. "I'll turn around."

"Yes, you will," I said tightly.

I hurried over to my dresser and grabbed a pair of fresh black leggings and an oversized sweatshirt. My underwear drawer was closer to Alec than I wanted to be. Flushed with embarrassment I walked over to it, knowing that he watched me out of the corner of his eye.

My hand touched the black victoria secret panties, just as Alec coughed.

"Do you mind?" I said tersely.

"I like the pink better."

Patience. Patience. Is this what its like to have a brother? No, that would be a no. Because it's illegal and icky to want a member of your family the way I want Alec.

Demetri. I needed to focus on Demetri.

I snatched the black pair just to piss Alec off and grabbed my sports bra from the other corner of the room.

"Girls take forever to get dressed," he grumbled, still looking away from me.

"Not usually, I'm just doing it for your benefit."

"You're crabby when you don't eat."

I sighed. "Okay, done."

He turned around, his gaze hungrily taking in my sweats as if I was wearing some sort of short dress. Alec nodded and looked toward the dinner. "I didn't really know what you wanted, so I threw in some stir fry with your leftover chicken, hope that's okay."

"Smells good." My stomach grumbled on cue as I walked over to the bed and sat down. "Aren't you going to eat?"

"Nat, I don't think I'll have an appetite for a week. I was too worried to do anything except call you and stare out the window."

"I was fine." I shoveled more food in my mouth.

"I promised Demetri."

I dropped the fork onto the plate. "You promised Demetri? What exactly did you promise him?"

Alec shrugged and looked away. "I promised him I'd take care of you. Then in my first day of babysitting you disappear."

"So I'm a toddler?"

"No, you're just very important."

"Important or irritating?"

"I'll tell you when I know." He gave an amused chuckle and pointed to the food. "All of it, Nat. Eat all of it."

"I swear you're trying to fatten me up."

"Maybe." He sat on the bed.

I ate in silence. Too hungry to be angry that Alec was watching me every time I lifted the fork to my mouth and swallowed. I swear, if I pretended to choke I'd probably give him gray hair.

"Done," I announced, wiping my mouth with the napkin he brought up.

"Good girl." He pushed the tray away. "Now, how about a rematch?"

"Rematch?"

"Last I remember..." He stretched out across my bed. "You cheated during our final round of Go Fish. I think I deserve a rematch, don't you?"

"Fine," I grumbled. "But I don't know how I'm going to manage to eat candy after all that food."

"I'll be easy on you."

"Right, you and easy don't really fit in the same sentence, Alec."

His lips twitched like he wanted to smile but thought better of it. "My place or yours?"

"Your place doesn't have crazy people coming in and out all hours of the night to talk about their feelings with my mom, so I choose yours."

He nodded and bounced off the bed. "You know just because they're seeking help from your mom doesn't make them crazy."

"I know. Otherwise I'd be putting you and your brother in that very same boat."

"I thought we were captains of the crazy boat. My mistake." Alec opened the bedroom door and I followed him down the creaky stairs.

"Why do you see her?"

Alec paused on the middle of the stairs, not turning around. I saw his shoulders tense. "We're just dealing with some stuff, that's all. You're mom's good at what she does. She wouldn't be one of the most renowned psychiatrists on the West Coast if she wasn't."

"Pardon?" My heart started to beat erratically, what was he talking about? "What did you just say?"

He turned around slowly his eyes not meeting mine. "Your mom, she comes very highly recommended."

"By who?" I yelled.

"Everyone." He shrugged. "Look, I thought you knew. Your mom's like a genius, she's written articles on grief, loss, depression, and addiction. I mean, I wouldn't be surprised if she's gotten offers to start her own rehab facility."

"Oh." I wasn't sure if I was more angry or guilty that I didn't know all of these things. Why hadn't she told me? Why wasn't I important enough to tell? If she was so freaking good at her job why did she ignore her own kid?

I felt my body slowly slump to the stairs. I hung my head in my hands and began to sob like a little girl.

Why couldn't I be enough for her? Why wasn't I important enough for her to at least say hi to? I had a rock star who had only known me for a few months calling my phone like I died, and my own mom still hadn't checked on me to make sure I made it home safely.

"Nat, don't cry. I'm so sorry." I was in Alec's arms in an instant. "Lets go to my house, okay? I'll make you hot chocolate and even let you win."

I hated that winning a game against him cheered me up, but it was enough to stop the tears.

I hated feeling insecure. Alec rubbed my arms as I sniffled a little more. "I just don't get how I don't even know my own family. I mean, am I that invisible?"

Alec tensed, his hands stopped rubbing my arms. "Nat, look at me."

My lower lip quivered as I locked eyes with him.

"You are anything but invisible. You are a treasure. I know your mom knows that. She loves you. Sometimes parents just suck at connecting with their kids."

"She sucks big time."

Alec laughed and kissed my cheek. "Yes, she does, but communication works both ways. Have you ever even asked her about work?"

Guilt lodged itself quite uncomfortably against my chest making it hard to breathe a bit. "No ,but..."

"Sorry to say, but that's how relationships work. One of you has to take the first step."

I sighed and nodded my head.

"Wait here." He set me on my feet and knocked quietly on my mom's office door. I wanted to run and hide. I couldn't face her. If she saw me crying she'd go all psychiatrist on me and I couldn't handle being psychoanalyzed now, not now, not when I needed her most. I couldn't handle the rejection of her telling me she had another client and we would talk later when I was calmer and she wasn't busy.

My fingers twitched in my palm as I clenched my hands tighter and tighter. The door opened. Alec stepped out, followed by my mom.

Crap.

"Are you okay, Honey?" She said *Honey*. I wanted to cry.

"I'm fine," I said, sending a glare in Alec's direction.

She looked at me for a minute then back at Alec. "I guess it's okay, just make sure she gets to bed at a decent time. Did you know she was sick?"

"He knew, mom." I clenched my teeth to keep from shouting, *He took care of me when you weren't here!*

"Okay, goodnight Sweetie. Have fun."

With that, the door closed behind her, my mouth dropped open in shock. "Did you just ask my mom if we could have a sleepover?"

"Of course not." Alec laughed.

My shoulders slumped in relief.

"I asked her if you could come play at my house and if you were really good, could you stay the night in my bed."

"You've got to be kidding me."

Alec's face lit up with a smile. "Only slightly. I did tell her we were going to hang out and not to wait up for you."

"Oh."

Why do I feel myself blushing?

"But if you want to spend the night, I wouldn't be opposed to it."

My heart began to thump wildly in my chest. These feelings I had for him were so wrong!

"You can have Demetri's room. He'd love nothing more than to come home and have your scent all over his sheets."

"Right." Irritated that my mind first went to spending the night in Alec's arms, and not to Demetri's bed, I bit my lip and looked at the floor. "So, Go Fish?"

"Absolutely."

I followed Alec out the door and into his house. It was impossible for me not to feel like I was being watched. I mean it had been a really weird couple of days, but Alec assured me that the security around the place had been upped, meaning even my place had cameras around. Not to mention giant bodyguards doing perimeter checks every few minutes. I blocked away the memories of the night Alec held me in his arms while I was sick, and stored them somewhere in the back of my psyche along with the searing kiss from Alec.

I had to keep those feelings hidden. I feared that if I, for one second, allowed myself to dwell on them, Demetri would be lost to me, and if Demetri was lost, then Alec would be too.

Chapter Eighteen

"Nat? Did you hear me?" Alec stepped in front of me bracing my shoulders with his hands. "Are you sure you're okay?"

"Fine." I gave a smile that I'm sure told him I wasn't anywhere near fine, but it worked. Wordlessly he led me to the living room and began setting out the game.

"So, what were you saying about letting me win?" I asked once the cards were dealt. Alec cursed from across the table, my grin grew wider, and I felt remarkably better.

"I thought you'd forget."

"You thought wrong."

Alec slammed down his first card. "Do you really want to win that way, Nat? Where I suck on purpose so you feel better about yourself?"

I thought about it for a minute. The way the Swedish fish would look on his face, his handsome grin erupting into annoyance at the idea that he was losing.

"Yes. Yes, I do."

"How did I know you were going to say that?" he grumbled and poured the fish onto the table. "Why don't I just eat two handfuls and then we can play like normal human beings?"

"Only if you intend on allowing me to lick them and put them on your face. There are rules you know and a promise is a promise."

I couldn't help the laughter as he looked at the Swedish fish then back at me, then back at his cards.

"Fifteen fish."

"Twenty."

"Seventeen and not a fish more!"

I sighed. "Deal."

Alec picked up one fish and licked it.

"Oh, no, no, no, I don't believe that's how the game's played." Without really thinking about it I plopped down next to him and put a fish in my mouth, getting it nice and sloppy, then very carefully placed it on his cheek.

Alec's eyes darkened at the contact. I tried to look away, but I couldn't. His eyes were so green, I felt lost in them, lost in the stupid moment.

The fish fell off of his cheek.

And just like that the spell was broken.

I instantly regretted moving to his side of the couch. His thigh was warm against mine. We reached for the next Swedish fish at the same time.

"Maybe a game isn't the best idea?" Alec blurted.

I nodded, because for once I was in total agreement with him.

"TV?"

"Sure!" I tucked my knees on the couch and watched as he flipped on the TV.

Wonder of all wonders, Demetri's face popped on. Entertainment News was doing a story on his current work with the underprivileged kids. Cameras flashed as he went into his hotel. His plane must have landed a few hours ago.

Guilt gnawed on me like a piranha and I could have

sworn I heard Alec curse aloud. It was as if the universe was reminding us not to be complete idiots. It was just a stupid attraction, nothing more! Plus, I had this ridiculous habit of always being vulnerable around Alec, which made him turn into the hero and me the damsel, and really what girl wouldn't be attracted to that?

Satisfied that I had yet again talked myself out of opening that secret place in my brain that stored all of the memories shared with Alec, I smiled at the TV. "He looks happy."

"Happiest I've seen him in a while," Alec said quietly.

And again with the guilt. We both sat awkwardly watching the entire report. Pictures of Demetri and Alec on tour, and then it panned to their current whereabouts in Seaside.

I was horrified to see the infamous picture of me and Alec's almost kiss, and then immediately the story went to a few pictures of me and Demetri holding hands and the kissing outside the restaurant.

It was weird watching myself on TV. But even stranger to actually be sitting by one of the objects of my desire, knowing that I was caught in that very sick love triangle.

Alec twitched beside me. His thigh just barely grazing mine. A commercial popped on the screen but still neither of us moved.

"It's late," he said softly.

"I know."

"We should go to bed."

I opened my mouth to speak but he interrupted.

"Separately."

"Right." I got to my feet and waited while Alec turned off the TV as well as the rest of the lights. Once the last light downstairs was extinguished, my agony as well as blood pressure heightened.

"Alec?" I called, because I couldn't see a thing in their house. It was pitch black and I still didn't know where I was going. I'd never in all this time been to Demetri's room, only Alec's.

"I'm here." His breath was hot on my neck, his hands slowly moved to my back and he guided me out of the living room and toward the stairs. Everywhere he touched felt like a livewire, even though I know he was only trying to be helpful. I stumbled on the final stair.

"You okay?" He chuckled.

No. I wanted to scream, *No!* But I didn't. Instead I nodded mutely, forgetting that he couldn't really see me, and waited while he walked in front of me and then grabbed my arm to tug me behind him.

We walked down to the end of the hall where his room was located, but instead of going to the left we went to the right.

"So…" Alec pushed open the door and flicked on the light. It wasn't at all what I expected it to be. The room had muted colors of khaki and white. His bed was a large king with a navy blue duvet and a ton of fluffy pillows. The windows were wide and facing the ocean. All in all, it felt more like a hotel than a guy's bedroom.

"Creepy, I know," Alec said behind me. "He's weird about keeping his room clean and clutter free, says it messes with his music if he has clutter in his life."

"Sounds like him." I smiled. I really did miss that boy.

"So," Alec clapped his hands together as if he was a tour guide making and important point, "The bathroom's right through there, and the sheets are clean. I'll see you in the morning, okay?"

"Okay."

Alec nodded and walked out of the room.

I called after him. "Alec, thanks for letting me stay and for…" I sighed. "For saying I'm important."

"No problem." He gave a sad smile and closed the door behind him.

I let out a sigh of relief as I slumped onto Demetri's bed. I really wished he was there. If he was there then his stupid brother wouldn't be distracting me like he was. Or at least I could lock myself in his room and pretend that his very attractive very unattainable brother wasn't across the hall from me.

The problem was, now that I was alone in their house, all I really wanted to do was tip toe across the hall and climb into Alec's bed. I mean it wasn't that I wanted to do anything, I just hated being alone, and he knew that.

Just as I was getting brave enough to go knock on his door and beg to sleep on the floor, the thunder rattled the windows. With a yelp I jumped into bed and threw the covers over my head like a little kid.

I must have fallen asleep, because the next thing I knew, something was chasing me. I was running toward Demetri. His face was filled with so much fear, and then I looked behind me and a car was coming around the corner.

Demetri screamed. I screamed and everything went black.

"No! No!" I jolted awake.

"Nat! Nat, wake up, Sweet. Wake up." Alec tenderly took me into his arms and rocked me gently. "It was just a dream."

My hands shook as he tried to pull me to a sitting position in his lap. I buried my head in his chest. His smell was such a comfort to me. I felt stupid for trembling, but I couldn't help but feel like my dream was somehow prophetic.

No matter how I looked at it.

I was going to hurt Demetri.

"Nat? Talk to me, Nat." Alec's voice shook.

I shivered. "It was so real."

"Do you want to talk about it?" He caressed my head, keeping it firmly tucked under his chin.

"No." My body convulsed again.

"Come on." Alec lifted me into his arms. I noticed his

chest was bare as I completely wrapped my arms around his neck. He was warm and comforting. The outline of his tattoos was dark in the moonlight. He brought me into his room and hit the door closed with his foot.

"What are you doing?" I asked, suddenly fearful that my dream was hitting too close to home. I couldn't be with Alec. I was with Demetri. I couldn't hurt him like this.

"Relax." Alec placed me on his bed and very carefully pulled back the covers. Exhausted, I snuggled into his pillow, savoring his scent.

He kissed my forehead and crawled in beside me. "Sleep, Nat."

I wanted to sleep. But how does a person sleep when she's emotionally cheating on her boyfriend with his brother? I shivered again, hating myself almost as much as I hated the nightmare.

"Come here." Alec draped an arm around me and tucked me into the curve of his body. My head fit perfectly beneath his chin. His breathing was so calm, so even. How was that possible when my heart was actually ready to take flight? The material of his pajama bottoms tickled my legs. I had stolen a pair of running shorts and a T-shirt from Demetri's dresser, and again the guilt stabbed me in the heart.

I wasn't sure if it was Alec reading my mind or just being really perceptive, but he grunted, "Nat, I'm exhausted and most of all I'm a good guy. Close your eyes, and stop worrying. Demetri would understand."

"Okay," I said in a small voice then my eyes fluttered closed.

The heat of the sun woke me up. Groggily I moved just slightly trying to stretch, but I couldn't move.

My body was pinned beneath Alec's. Our legs entangled with each other in such an intimate way that I'm sure I was blushing to the roots of my hair. I tried to pull out from underneath him, but if anything his arms tightened around me. Dang his eyelashes were long. Black against tan skin and his constant five o'clock shadow. I didn't notice before, but there was a small tattoo near the back of his ear that trailed down his neck onto his back. I leaned in closer, trying not to laugh as his lips parted slightly and then his eyebrows furrowed as if he was having a dream.

He was gorgeous.

Not yours, Nat. Not your gorgeous, I reminded myself as I pushed up on my elbow and peeked at his tattoo.

"Stop inspecting me, it's creepy," Alec said in a hoarse voice that I found so dead sexy, I was paralyzed. His eyes fluttered open, vibrant green pools of beauty stared back at me. "Did I mention I haven't slept that good in years?"

"I'm the best bed partner ever." I joked trying to nudge him, instead, my nudge made it so I fell back onto the bed rather forcefully. I had forgotten our legs were intertwined. The action made it so that our bodies fell together.

Alec closed his eyes and cursed. When he opened them again, they were full of steely resolve. Man, this guy was good. Not that I thought I was any kind of prize, but if he truly was trying to keep his hands off, he deserved to be sainted.

"Nat, we should, um, go for a run."

"Okay."

Neither of us moved.

My breathing grew faster as his eyes fell to my lips and then, in a flash, those same green eyes darkened.

I couldn't stop him, even if I wanted to.

His head descended, and I didn't care that I was alone with him, that Demetri was gone, that this was wrong. I was lost in him, and I never wanted to come back.

His lips touched mine. I wanted to cry out in frustration when he pulled back. I reached up and tugged his head down.

With a groan he pinned my hands to the bed and threw his other leg over my body, straddling me with his weight. He tasted so good, so warm. His kiss was so different than

Demetri's, it was the only kiss I could compare it to. Where Demetri was playful, Alec was aggressive. Where Demetri had nipped teasingly, Alec possessed.

He wrapped his hands around me, pulling me against him as his tongue pushed deeper into my mouth. This was a guy that was experienced, that much was certain. I wrapped my legs tighter around him, making his body one with mine as I gave into the kiss with everything in me. It didn't matter that it was morning, that I was cheating, that it was so horribly wrong. All I could taste was him, and all I wanted was him.

He sucked my lower lip, then bit it and with a curse pushed away, his eyes closed as he lifted himself from me and cursed. "I'm sorry, Nat."

Every muscle was flexed as he sat on the edge of the bed. His back was ramrod straight, his arms clenching the sheets.

"Why are you always apologizing after kissing me?" I asked, slowly moving to sit next to him.

He laughed bitterly. "Because I shouldn't be kissing you, Nat."

"But I thought you liked me."

"Liked you?" Alec nearly shouted. I backed up. I didn't like seeing him mad, he was normally in such control of his emotions that I didn't know how to respond to him. "I don't just like you, Nat. But it doesn't matter."

"Why?"

"He loves you, Nat."

"I..." I didn't know what to say. "I care for Demetri, you know I do."

Alec swallowed and looked away, his Adam's apple bobbing in his throat as if he was trying to keep from shouting again.

"I just care about you too."

"Damn it! Do you have any idea how screwed up this is, Nat?"

I nodded, my shoulders slumped. I was so tired of

fighting my feelings. So tired of telling myself I had to choose or I would lose them both.

"It won't happen again." He swore. "I promised him it wouldn't happen again."

"What do you mean? Why are you so cryptic?"

Alec bit his lower lip and then let out a long sigh. "I would lose much more than your friendship if I answered that question, and regardless of my actions around you, I still truly desire to be your friend."

"Can you? With this between us?" I was grasping at straws. I needed him to admit it wasn't just me. That I wasn't going absolutely bat shit crazy.

He was quiet for a few minutes. It felt like hours when he finally answered, "I have to."

"So that's that?" I said angrily.

Alec stood and turned to face me. "Yes. End of discussion."

I glared but he stood firm. What was with him and his need for control? "Fine, let's go for a run."

"Nat." He reached out and grabbed my hand. "Please don't be mad. I don't think I could handle it if I knew you were mad. I know you don't get it, but we're messed up, both of us. My brother and I. You're the only one that's been able to bring him out of it. He needs you."

"More than you do?" I whispered looking down at the floor.

Alec cursed. "No."

Surprised by his answer my head jolted up.

"I just know at what cost it would be to have you, and it's not a sacrifice I'm willing to make."

Tears threatened to pour down my face at his admission. I nodded, my lower lip quivering. I turned around as quick as I could, warm salty tears poured down my cheeks. I hadn't expected his second rejection to hurt worse than the first, but it did. Somehow my heart felt like it was ripping in two, and I couldn't fight the slight tremble in my hands as I wiped the tears away.

"Don't cry," Alec said moving behind me and pulling my body back against his. "I promise this is for the best. He can make you so happy, Nat. He deserves to be happy. You love him, I know you do."

I nodded and without looking at him answered, "I love you, too."

Chapter Nineteen

Alec's arms tensed around me. Had I really just said that out loud? I was embarrassed enough that I was crying. I expected him to recoil from me, to shout, or even curse. Instead his lips grazed my ear. "I love you, too."

I shuddered in his arms. He released me. "No more, Nat. We can't talk about this anymore, okay?"

I turned around, the stain of tears were still present on my cheeks. I nodded and exhaled. "We should run."

He seemed thankful for the subject change, his eyes widened briefly and then he nodded. "Yeah, um… let me just get my stuff on. Want me to meet at your house in about ten minutes?"

"Sure." I gave him the most cheerful smile I could conjure up and bolted out the door. I ran the entire way to my house. I only had a few minutes and I needed those minutes like I needed air.

Once I was inside my bedroom, I slammed the door behind me, fell to my knees and wept.

True to his word, ten minutes later Alec was outside knocking on the door. I splashed my face with water and grabbed my phone and ear buds.

I didn't look any worse for the wear. He was a boy, but he wasn't a complete idiot. He'd know I would cry, so it shouldn't surprise him all that much.

"Ready?" he asked the minute I opened the door.

"Yup." I gave him a cheerful smile and prayed silently that I would make it through the run without having a complete breakdown.

After the first mile, the familiar strain in my legs began anew, helping me refocus on my breathing and pace rather than on the ache in my chest from this morning. My mind flashed to Alec in bed, our bodies entwined, our kiss heated. It was like nothing I had ever experienced mainly because my response to him was so different — primal even. I craved more, needed more from him.

Whatever they were hiding must be big. The bond they had with one another was scary strong, almost as if they both had some traumatic experience and lived through it. The only thing I could think of was their father having cancer. I can't imagine.

At mile four, we were getting ready to turn back when Demetri's voice came over the speakers. I smiled and looked at Alec.

"What?" he asked.

"One of your songs. Demetri's singing," I said.

Alec smiled. "He's talented."

And that was it. We both stood there looking at one another with sadness, love, friendship, and secrets. I took everything we shared and again stored it into that tiny place in my brain where I labeled the box *Alec*. It could have said *first love* on it, but I was *lucky* enough to have two loves in my life, and the choice had been taken from me by the very boy who had *forever* reflecting in his eyes.

"Race you back?" I grinned.

"Don't trip," Alec teased and pushed me before taking

off.

Tears blurred my vision as I chased after him. It was too close to a metaphor for my current situation in life. I would never reach him, never have him, and if I was lucky enough to catch him for even one second, he would always run.

Odd, that in the end Demetri would be the safe one. The one I could trust with my heart.

****

"Nat, hurry up!" Alesha shouted from downstairs.

I rolled my eyes at the reflection in the mirror and put in my earrings. The guys won their football game, and we were quickly trying to get ready for the dance. We had to be there earlier than everyone else so we could take tickets and make sure nobody snuck in alcohol or kids from other schools. "Coming!" I fired back, grabbing my shoes from the box on the bed and skipping down the stairs.

Alec was at the bottom talking with Evan. They were both in black slacks and nice shirts, but it was Alec who stood out. Of course he would wear all black. His clothes screamed expensive, you could actually see the thread count difference between his shirt and Evan's, and I was a few feet away from them.

"Wow!" Evan applauded. "You clean up well, Nat."

I rolled my eyes and looked to Alec for approval. His mouth was set in a grim line. I tilted my head to the side and cleared my throat. "Does my date approve?"

"Yes." His voice was hoarse, his eyes dark, he looked away and licked his lips.

Alesha grabbed my hand. "Okay, got everything you need? Because we needed to be there like ten minutes ago!"

"Yup." I put on a pair of flip flops and held my shoes in my hand. No way was I going to wear those babies all night.

We rode in Alec's car, because there really was no use

renting a limo when your date has such a cool ride.

My phone buzzed.

HV FN 2NITE, BBY. MISS U SO MCH! –D

I smiled and texted him back.

MISS U 2! I DN'T THNK UR BRO LKS MY DRESS. ☺

WHT? U'D LK GD N ANYTHNG. TK A PIC & SND IT 2 ME.

"Evan, can you take a picture?" I asked slyly and posed for the camera. I quickly sent it to Demetri and waited.

My alert went off.

DAMN. I H8 MY BRO RT NOW. TELL HIM 2 KP HIS DRTY HNDS OFF.

Guilt stabbed me in the chest. I needed to reassure him.

NO WRRIES! MISS U SO MCH. COME HME SN?

He replied instantly.

PROMISE.

I sighed and put the phone back in my clutch. Alec hadn't said two words since we got into the car. Maybe he was just trying to keep his distance. I couldn't blame him. After our run the day before, we had gone our separate ways and said perhaps three words to each other before meeting up for Homecoming. It just seemed easier to avoid everything.

We pulled up to the school parking lot. Music was already booming from inside. We rushed in, Alesha went to the tickets, and Alec and I were put on door patrol.

After ten minutes we realized that it wouldn't work. Too many kids were excited to see Alec and almost every single girl that walked by blatantly ignored her date, all with looks in their eyes that said, "I'll drop him in a second if you smile at me."

Alec was polite but I could tell it was wearing on him. I snuck up behind Alesha. "Hey can we switch?"

"Sure, I'm almost done anyway."

Alec and I took her seats and managed to be civil to one another, though each time one of us reached for money or tickets, our hands would graze and the storage in my brain would threaten to explode. If I didn't get a handle on it I was going to literally throw myself onto him. How embarrassing.

It was just because I was missing Demetri so much, too.

Alec was cool and distant once we sold the last ticket. We were at our max. It was up to security to keep kids out and keep others in. Luckily, Bob and Lloyd agreed to help, considering that it was a security threat to have Alec running around with all the normal kids.

"Do you want to dance?" I asked shyly once we walked into the gym.

Alec grinned and tugged me toward the dance floor. He may be brooding, he may be indifferent, he may have possibly broken my heart twice, but the man could dance.

He was amazing.

I felt like I had two left feet next to him.

I kept apologizing when I felt like I couldn't keep up. He rolled his eyes and laughed, then pulled me so I was nearly on top of him, his hips swirling seductively. Even if my brain wasn't coordinated to figure out what to do, my body did. Instinctively, I joined in and within minutes we had a crowd around us. The song turned to a popular AD2 song that had a techno tango feel to it.

The music video had millions of hits on Youtube alone, not to mention the people who did parodies or their own flash mobs to it.

It had been filmed at a high school.

And suddenly it dawned on me, as the lights darkened even more and a spotlight shone on us, that I was in my own music video.

Alec grabbed a hat from some random guy and did this crazy Justin Bieber/Michael Jackson move that had people screaming until they were hoarse, and then he jerked me flush against him, lifting my leg above his hip and dipped me backwards. With ease he twisted me around him and we were doing a tango. Which, lucky for me, was the only dance I ever actually learned.

As seductively as possible, I twisted to the ground and skimmed my heeled foot in between his legs, kicking to the right and left before turning and standing. Once my back was to him his arms moved slowly down my shoulders and then down my stomach as he grabbed my legs and wrapped them backwards around him.

The sensation of dancing with him was unlike anything I had ever experienced.

The song ended. We were both winded. People clapped. My laughter broke the spell. It had to be the most fun I'd ever had in my entire life. For once, Alec joined in, his face coming alive with joy. I'm sure it stunned everyone else just as much as it stunned me. He was gorgeous, absolutely perfect. No guy should be that good-looking.

"I think I may have a crush on this Alec," I joked.

"This Alec?" He looked confused, sweat trickled down the side of his face. Dang, it was hot.

"The one who seduces girls on the dance floor and puts Justin Bieber to shame… hey, um, can I have your autograph?" I fluttered my eyelashes.

His mouth gaped open and then he cursed. "You suck."

I was still kind of in his arms, we both threw our heads back and laughed, he twirled me twice and then tugged my body against his again.

The music switched to a slow song. I put my head on his chest. He sighed heavily and we finished the dance in silence.

"Nat, I—"

The lights flickered, interrupting his thought.

A knowing grin spread across his face. "I'll be right back."

And just like that he left me alone on the dance floor.

The principal walked to the microphone and tapped it twice, causing an ear-splitting sound to emanate from the speakers. "Sorry about that, folks. The dancing will recommence after this special performance." He cleared his throat and looked around the crowd. "It is my pleasure to announce, AD2!"

Everyone screamed. Everyone but me. Demetri? Was he back? Why didn't he tell me? What was he doing?

The stage went dark.

And then lit up like a Christmas tree. Demetri was standing in the middle of it. My heart thumped wildly in my chest. I hadn't realized how much I missed him. I wanted to run onto the stage and tackle him.

"Nat," his voice rumbled in the microphone. "This one's for you."

Alec was suddenly behind him with a guitar, a microphone in front of his face too.

The tune was haunting. Not at all like their usual techno beats. Everyone in the room began to sway with the slow beat.

"Torn Like Rain," Alec said into the microphone not once taking his eyes off of me.

Brown eyes, blond hair, I can't help but stare. She's got me hypnotized. I need her, like oxygen, I can't explain the way she makes me feel inside. Like rain, washing my fears away, she makes me feel like I can say all those things I'm too scared to say.

Breathe in, breathe out, sometimes you just gotta shout your love. Shout your love. Inhale, exhale, the beauty of your love will always be enough. Enough.

I watched as Demetri's lips moved the words into the atmosphere of the room. Everyone was silent, just as transfixed as I had been the first moment I read the lyrics. As expected, it was Alec who sang the bridge. His voice was so different than Demetri's, yet they complimented each other so well.

His eyes never left mine as he sang *come back to me*. I wanted to hate him for staring at me, for trying to convey to me some secret message of his desire to have me but his stupid inability to do so.

I didn't know I had been staring at him, or that anyone had seen.

My eyes flickered back to Demetri. He saw the entire thing. As if it spurred him on even more, he belted out the final part of the chorus. Tears stung at the back of my eyes.

When they were done, it was impossible to hear yourself think. People went crazy. They wouldn't stop clapping.

And then both Alec and Demetri were gone.

"May I have this dance?" Demetri whispered in my ear from behind me.

I turned around and threw my arms around his neck. "Why didn't you tell me you were coming?"

"I wasn't sure I could." Demetri held me in his arms and kissed me softly across the mouth. "I found out around noon that I could make it up here, but I've gotta fly back out in a few hours."

"You flew here for me?" I gulped.

Demetri laughed and nuzzled my neck. "I would do anything for you. Don't you see that already?"

Guilt flared in my chest again, my eyes were swimming with tears, and then I saw Alec across the room. He gave a slight nod as if giving permission and I hated him for it. I hated him and loved him so much it hurt.

How did this happen in the real world? I always laughed at people who said they liked more than one guy at the same time. Well, what about love? Nobody could tell me what I was feeling wasn't real. If anything, it was too real, too much, and so fast. I felt like I was drowning.

What do you do when you're drowning but the only way to be free is to hold on to the one thing in all the world you're afraid won't be able to keep both of you afloat? That was how I viewed Demetri. He was all over the place, unreadable, uncontrollable.

I sighed heavily into his chest.

"Baby, what's wrong?" Demetri laughed and kissed my forehead.

I shrugged. "I just miss you, that's all."

"I miss you, too." His eyes brightened as his mouth descended and covered mine. His kiss was welcome. It helped me forget Alec. I kissed him back, hard, as hard as I could without mauling him on the dance floor.

He groaned, his arms coming around me, and then he was lifting me and twirling me in circles as he kissed me.

"Can we go?" I asked when he pulled back.

"Are you sure?" he looked nervous, his eyes glancing at all the people around us. I needed to be with him. Alone. I needed confirmation that this was right, what we were doing was right.

"Yes."

"Your carriage awaits." He tucked my arm within his and escorted me out of the gym. The late October air bit at my face and I hid in the safety of Demetri's arms.

I jumped in the car and was ridiculously grateful that my boyfriend had heated seats. I turned mine on full blast and shivered.

"You look hot tonight, Nat." Demetri gave me a seductive grin that I felt all the way down to my toes as we drove out of the parking lot.

"Where are we going?"

"Where do you want to go?"

I shrugged. "I just want to be with you."

Demetri's face relaxed as he drove down the street toward home. "Good, I want that too."

The house was dark when we drove up. I looked for any other cars but Alec hadn't come back from the dance yet.

Nervous, I unbuckled my seatbelt and followed Demetri up the stairs. He threw the keys on the counter and grabbed my hand.

"I heard you slept in my bed," he murmured into my hair as he pushed open his door.

"It's possible." I grinned, shielding my mind from the memory of the nightmare.

"Did you wear my clothes too?"

"Yup."

He groaned. "Ah, you are killing me, girl." His fingers were threading through my hair. "You're so damn beautiful, Nat. And you don't even know it. You don't see what everyone else sees. This beautiful, bright girl — you're like the sun."

"The sun?" I repeated.

"I want to revolve around you."

Whoa, that's bordering on very serious and possessive. Demetri stumbled a bit as he tugged at my hair. His mouth tasted like alcohol, had he been drinking before he sang? His mouth was on mine before I could protest. Nimble fingers found the back of my dress and began to unzip. I wasn't sure if I wanted to pull away or step further into his embrace. His tongue flicked my teeth and then plunged into my mouth, forcing me to either kiss him back or jerk away.

I kissed him back. I decided not to think as I curved my body into his and matched his kiss as best I could. Another moan escaped and I realized it was me. My dress dropped to the floor. I was freezing. This was too fast. What was I doing? He made me feel things, good things, but it was always so confusing with Demetri. I always had to think about it.

With Alec, it was easy.

And that was the problem.

With Demetri I had to rationalize, I had to plan ahead, I had to think. With Alec, thinking wasn't even possible. It was instinct.

"No." I pushed at Demetri's chest. He backed up and cursed.

"Sorry, Nat. I didn't mean to get out of control." He

looked almost horrified that my dress was off of me. Gone was the seducer of hundreds of women. "Nat, damn." Demetri tugged the dress back up and quickly zipped me. I'm sorry, I'm just used to more. I'm sorry."

Why was he apologizing so much? "Demetri, you're fine." I kissed him briefly on the cheek and pulled him into a hug. "It got out of hand, it's fine."

His eyes were filled with pain. He cursed and for some reason trembled beneath my touch. "What's wrong?"

"I just promised, that's all."

"You promised?"

He nodded. "Myself. I promised I wouldn't have sex with another girl unless I knew for sure."

"Knew what for sure?"

Okay, these boys were beyond secretive.

He swallowed and looked away. "You like him."

"Him?"

Demetri rolled his eyes and softly pushed me away. "Nat, I'm not stupid. We've alluded to this conversation many times before. It's always the same. I feel like I'm fighting this invisible battle, and you make it that much worse when you pretend to be ignorant."

"Alec," I breathed.

Demetri didn't look at me. "Has he kissed you?"

Goodbye, Alec. "Yes," I mumbled, wanting to be shot on the spot. "But, he told me he wasn't good for me, he pushed me away, we both decided we were better friends. It was a mistake."

The words were flying out of my mouth so fast I wasn't even sure he heard everything.

Demetri stared out the window a long time. "I just don't get it. I don't understand why it always has to be like this."

"Like what?" Maybe he would finally tell me what was bothering both of them so much. Starting with why they were here.

He shook his head. "I need to change, Nat. My flight leaves in an hour." He quickly peeled off his shirt. I gasped.

"What?" He braced my shoulders. "Are you okay?"

"Your, um, your tattoo." Forget similar. The tattoo was identical to Alec's. Hands held a heart within them and thought I didn't know Latin, the words looked the same. Why would they have the exact same tattoo? What did that mean? I touched it. He flinched as if in pain. "What does it say?"

Demetri exhaled and looked away. "My heart will be yours forever."

I choked back a sob as tears filled my eyes. "Just like Alec's."

His eyes flashed and then he grabbed my arm and pulled our bodies together until there was no space separating us. "I'm nothing like Alec."

What just happened? I tried to pull away but he held me firm in his grasp. "Please, Nat. I'm not him, I'm not him." Demetri closed his eyes and touched his forehead to mine. "I was never him. She knew that, but it didn't matter. I just want to be me. Love *me*."

"Did I ask you to be him?" I said weakly.

Demetri tilted my chin and brushed a soft kiss across my lips. "No, Baby. It's not what you said. This is all me, my shitty baggage. Got it?"

"Got it," I mumbled, though it was clear I really didn't get anything. I didn't understand his mood swings, why he was so secretive and why he would go all crazy saying he wasn't Alec.

"You okay?" I rubbed my hand across his smooth face then brought my lips to his. His kiss was hungry. He pushed me against the wall and again his nimble hands moved to my back to unzip my dress. Okay, what the heck? Déjà vu much? His skilled whorish hands had me out of my dress in seconds. It pooled at my feet. He lifted me off the ground and lifted my hips grabbing my butt in the process and making it impossible for me not to straddle him. I was still wearing my heels but only had my lingerie on. The very same lingerie that Alesha convinced me I should wear that night.

Demetri moaned as one of his hands held me in place while he pushed harder against me and began caressing the delicate lace of my bra. His hands were hot against my cool skin and even though it felt so good It was also all wrong.

"Demetri," I panted. "What's wrong? Remember, slow?" His kisses assaulted my senses as he swirled his tongue down the side of my neck. This was wrong. Something was terribly wrong. "Demetri," I repeated, this time trying to sound sterner. Yes, he was hot, and of course it felt good, I mean I'm in high school. I'm no saint. I mean, until this year I hadn't even been kissed, and now I felt like a giant hussy.

He groaned and began tugging on my panties. "No!" I didn't mean to shout, it just came out. His hands froze, he cursed and I nearly fell to the floor from the abruptness of his release.

"You need to go, Nat." He had his back turned to me.

"What the heck was that?" Goosebumps raised across my arms from the sudden chill in the room.

"Nothing."

"Demetri." I walked up behind him and wrapped my arms around his stomach. "Talk to me."

"I just wanted you first."

I blinked a few times trying to allow the information to digest into my fuzzy brain. "First?"

"Before everything happens." His rigid muscles were rippling with tension beneath my palms. I broke out into a cold sweat.

"What are you talking about? Are you high? On drugs? Before what happens?"

For as long as I live, I will never forget the look in Demetri's eyes. The way his pupils grew, almost dilating to the outside part of his blue irises. His mouth set in a grim line and his shoulders almost slumped as if he was in severe pain and didn't want to scream but would hold it in until it exploded, shattering him from the inside out.

I noticed his hand clench at his side, and then he brought it to my face and closed his eyes momentarily. Why was his hand shaking?

"I'll always love you," he whispered.

I put my hand over his holding it in place against my cheek. "Demetri, I love you." I needed him to know how I felt. And it was all true, I knew it was true. I'd never felt so strong for anyone except Alec, but this clearly wasn't the time or place to say something like that.

"I know." Demetri smiled sadly and exhaled. "I'll see you in another week or so, okay?"

"Okay." I shivered and went to put on my dress, then felt warm hands pull me back into a hug.

"I'll miss you," he croaked. I nodded numbly and watched him pop something into his mouth.

"What are you taking?"

"Pain killers," He rolled his eyes, "Because I'm in pain, Nat."

I waited for him to say something else but he just threw the prescription pills back onto the bed and turned to face me again. He bit his lip and pulled out his phone.

"Gotta go, Nat." He opened his mouth. I needed him to explain to me what was happening, but instead all I got was a, "I'll text you."

Why did it suddenly feel like I was dying? Why did my heart constrict as if he was saying goodbye?

I walked home in a haze of confusion. Forget Alec confusing me. Demetri took the cake in that arena. My heart felt sick, the kind of sick you get when you don't know whether you want to throw up or go lie down and have a good cry. I stumbled up the stairs to my room and lay down on my bed. After a few minutes my eyes felt heavy. I allowed myself to succumb to the darkness, which was really the problem in the first place, wasn't it? I allowed myself to succumb — to everything.

Chapter Twenty

Sunday came and went with nothing exciting to report other than the fact that my heart felt like lead, and every time I texted Demetri he refused to answer me. Odd, because he had always been really good about getting back to me when I chatted. But he was teaching, so it was possible he was super busy.

Later that night I was so viciously bored, considering my ultra-expensive phone wasn't buzzing at me, that I turned on TV.

Rumor has it that the D in band AD2 has been seen sneaking around town with someone other than his girlfriend. Our sources tell us that Anjelica Greene was spotted leaving the star's hotel room in the wee hours of the morning this morning with a very satisfied grin on that picture perfect face. Has the rock star dumped the local hottie? Stay tuned to find out!

What. The. Hell.

I threw the remote onto the couch and ran over to the guys' house. I lifted my hand to bang on the door when it suddenly flew open, revealing a very shirtless Alec. Well, no one ever said life was fair, or easy, or awesome.

"What the heck is his problem!" I roared, stomping into the house like a woman on the edge.

"Good evening to you too," Alec muttered behind me.

I ignored him. "First he's all trying to take advantage of me at your house, then spouting nonsense about you and me, and then…" I began to feel hysterical. "He said that he wanted to be first. Of course, that was after his second attempt at getting me out of my dress and into his bed, and then he wouldn't let me go, and then he got all weird and I saw pills and freaked. It was like he was saying goodbye. More like, *Sorry Nat, but I'm gonna go screw some movie star instead!*" I felt tears coming on but fought them back, allowing my anger to take over. "I've been heart-broken for almost forty-eight hours thinking I've done something tragic to him and he's, he's—"

"Nat," Alec interrupted, his voice severe. "Stop."

"No!" I whipped around and charged toward him, finally poking him in the chest. "You don't get to tell me what to do! You rejected me! Twice — wait, three times!"

Alec rolled his eyes. "Listen, Nat. As much as I'd love to sit here and listen to you complain about my brother's shitty decisions and lack of love for you, I'd rather not. Everything he's done has been for you, and you repay him by coming over here and talking shit? Really?"

"How is him cheating on me doing me a favor? Because I'm dying to know. This ought to be good." I crossed my arms and waited, finally allowing a tear to run down my cheek. I quickly wiped it away and broke eye contact, choosing to look at my Converse rather than Alec's shirtless perfection.

"It's complicated."

My head snapped up. "Of course it is. It's always complicated with you two, and you never tell me why! I don't know why you're here, I don't know why you chose my mom out of all people to see, and I don't know why you have the same stupid tattoo!"

"Get out," Alec snapped, pulling my arm.

"I didn't mean it was stupid, just that—"

"Out." Alec gently pushed me out his door and leaned against the frame. "Nat, go home. We should never have involved you in the first place."

"What are you saying?" I felt my lower lip quiver.

"I'm saying goodbye."

"You're shutting me out," I said numbly, not allowing my heart to believe that I had successfully lost the two boys I loved in the course of a weekend.

He closed his eyes while he whispered, "Family comes first."

"And I'm not family."

Silence.

"Right." I choked back a sob and ran back to my house.

I didn't know that I had been crying so loud. My mom pounded on my door and finally I opened it, probably looking like some crazy person with mascara-stained cheeks.

"Oh, Baby!" She embraced me and I cried even harder.

"What's wrong, Sweetie?"

Sweetie? Baby? She never said those things to me. I wanted to tense up, to recoil and pull back, this wasn't familiar for me, but I needed her comfort so much that I didn't care. I just wanted to be loved, by someone.

"Boys are so stupid." I shivered and wiped my nose with the sleeve of my sweatshirt.

Mom sighed. "Any boys in particular giving you grief?"

I nodded.

"Would these boys be my clients?"

I nodded again.

"Natalee." Mom's grip tightened on my arm as she held me cradled next to her body. "Those boys aren't normal."

"No crap, Mom."

Mom tensed next to me. "No, Nat, not like that. I mean they're so much more than they seem. Life has dealt them some pretty screwed up situations. They stick together because they're all they have. Does that make sense?"

"No." Well, kind of, but I was angry so I said no anyways.

Mom pushed back my hair and kissed me on the forehead. Seriously, someone beam me back to the planet, this was so foreign. "A year ago, they were dealt a very hard blow. The fact that they were able to even pull out of it is astonishing both to me and to everyone else who knows."

"Knows? As in, you know?"

"Confidentiality, Natalee," she reminded me.

I sighed.

"Anyway, I imagine if any of this involves you, then a grand dose of fear is also involved, and when you allow fear to rule your emotions and your choices, well, you end up pushing away those you love most."

I knew it well. Oh, how I knew it. I pushed my mom away, afraid that if I allowed myself to be attached that she would constantly reject me, because it seemed like she always did. But did she? Or did she just assume I was really happy and leave me alone to figure my own stuff out?

"I'm confused, my head hurts," I complained.

Mom laughed. "Why don't we go make some dinner?"

"We?" I repeated, my voice absolutely deadpan with sarcasm.

"I canceled the rest of the night."

I pulled away from her and looked into her tired eyes. "May I ask why?"

"One of your confused boys asked me to."

"Oh."

"Yeah, *oh*." She lifted an eyebrow. "Natalee, Sweetie, I didn't know."

I got up and tried to ignore the feeling of guilt and anger that washed over me. "What are you talking about?"

"I thought you were happy. If I would have known you wanted more, Honey, I would have given it to you. You're just always so closed off I thought you didn't need me, or anyone for that matter."

A sob erupted from my throat before I could stop it. I fell to my knees on the floor, my body violently shook from years of grief kept inside.

"Oh, Honey!" Mom swept down next to me and pulled me into her lap, rocking me back and forth like she did when I was little. "I'm so sorry! Can you forgive me? Oh sweetie, I'm so sorry!"

I nodded, but the tears wouldn't stop. Geez, you'd think someone really was dying.

By the time I stopped crying it was near midnight. We made a late night pizza and put on a movie. Just my mom and me. She promised she would try harder as long as I didn't push her away and put on the *I'm fine and independent* face. My dad wasn't due home tonight because of a late surgery, but mom promised she would talk to him when she could.

I went to sleep for the first time in years feeling like my parents cared, that they actually saw me. No longer was I invisible, and even though the rejection from both Alec and Demetri hurt, I felt confident. For the first time I was confident.

Apparently having a parent show affection did something to a person, because when I closed my eyes after crying all those tears and severely dehydrating myself, I fell asleep with a smile on my face.

****

My alarm was so loud I nearly had a heart attack when it went off. My legs were tangled in the sheets and I hadn't slept very well, considering I kept dreaming that Alec was in a car trying to run me over with it while Demetri stood by laughing.

I forced myself to expel their images from my mind, which of course meant that when I drove to school every radio station in the known universe was playing their songs. I flipped off the radio then passed a store that just happened to have their faces splashed across the windows.

Basically, I was ready to scream by the time I arrived at the school. I slammed my truck door and marched through the front doors, only to be met by mocking stares and smirks from the student body. Does nobody read anymore?

Alesha was by my locker. "Oh, my gosh, Nat! I'm so sorry about Demetri, do you need anything?" She touched my arm. I flinched.

"Nope, I'm fine. We're fine," I said through clenched teeth even though he still hadn't texted me back or answered my frantic calls. "It's just celebrity gossip, you know how that goes."

She nodded her head. "Yeah, of course. Well okay, I'm gonna go to class."

Did I mention that I can't lie to save my life?

I opened my locker and briefly contemplated attempting to climb into it, but it was twenty sizes too small, meaning I would have to become a contortionist in order to pull it off, and even then it would be uncomfortable. The bell rang. With a moan I put my head inside the locker, cursing all men for their inability to keep it in their pants and communicate like normal humans.

"Rough night?" Alec said behind me.

I flipped around so fast that my face came into contact with the metal door. It caught my lip, don't ask me how. "Ouch!"

"Damn it, Nat! Could you try not to trip or hurt yourself at least once?"

I glared as I patted my lip, blood trickling down my finger, "Yeah, because I like being hurt and making a complete fool out of myself."

Whoa, double meaning.

We both stood there glaring at one another. Finally, Alec

rolled his eyes and grabbed my hand, pulling me toward the women's restroom.

"Alec, what are you—"

He pushed through the doors dragging me behind him. "Everyone decent?"

No answer.

He kicked open all the stall doors then went to the sink and wet a paper towel.

"Alec, you can't just—"

"Stop. Talking." He held up the paper towel to my cut. I flinched from the sting of the water hitting the open wound and tried to pull back, but his grip on my chin kept me firmly in place. "What am I going to do with you, Nat?"

"Is that a rhetorical question," I mumbled as he wiped away the blood.

"Not anymore." He shook his head, a small smile playing at the corner of his lips.

"I don't know." I sighed. "But I'm going to be late for class."

"I got it."

"You got it?" I lifted an eyebrow. "As in, you got the teacher in your pocket, or you're going to tell them I got in a fight with the locker and lost?"

"Just don't worry about it."

"Good to know you're still as confusing as ever."

"Why, Nat, was that a compliment?"

My teeth clenched.

He chuckled and threw the paper towel away. "All better. Come on."

And again I was getting dragged through the hallways like a little kid on her first day of school. We reached my class and Alec literally pushed me through the door.

Every head in the classroom turned in our direction.

"I'll be sitting in on this one, Mr. Smith," Alec said, guiding me to the back of the room toward two empty seats.

"I don't need a babysitter," I snapped once we took our seats.

"Obviously." His eyes flickered to my cut lip.

I looked away and closed my eyes in annoyance. He was still acting like he was extremely offended by my presence, so why did he help me when I was hurt? I looked at him from the corner of my eye. He appeared to be genuinely interested in what the teacher was saying, his concentration was intense.

I kept my gaze on him, not hearing a word the teacher said. His chin was set in a firm line as if he was clenching his teeth but didn't even realize he was doing it. The muscles flexed in his jaw. I was captivated as I watched his skin ripple down his neck. Black hair fell over his face, his long eyelashes blinking against his high cheekbones. He was so different than Demetri. So dark, and yes, still brooding. My eyes fell to his muscled arms now tucked beneath one another making him look more cut than usual. His feet were crossed at the ankles and his legs stretched out in front of him.

I wasn't sure how long I stared at him, but it felt like minutes when the bell rang, ushering us out of the room and into second period.

"Nat, you should probably be less obvious next time."

"Next time?" I repeated breathlessly. Yes, it's possible I was still thinking about his arms and the way they bulged under his too perfect T-shirt.

"Next time you check me out for an entire class period."

I felt myself blush. "I wasn't…"

"You were."

I gave him a stern look.

He shrugged and grabbed my messenger bag from my arm.

"I can carry that."

He shrugged and kept walking. "I know."

Aggravating did not even begin to describe the guy. By the time the lunch bell rang he had successfully followed me to every class, in his defense — not that I felt like defending his behavior — he had at least two out of the three classes with me, but still. It was bordering on ridiculous.

I ignored him as I walked through the lunch line. My stomach was in knots so nothing looked appetizing. By the time I reached the end of the line my tray was still empty.

"Eat," Alec said behind me.

I rolled my eyes so he couldn't see me and turned around ready to do battle. "I'm not hungry."

"You still need food."

"Are we really going to sit here and argue?"

Alec grabbed my empty tray. "Of course not."

I exhaled in relief, but it was short-lived as I watched him go back through the line and pile my tray high with every single option on the hot lunch list. He paid for the food and brought me the tray. I swear it was bending from the weight of food.

"Please tell me we're sharing," I grumbled.

Alec smirked and took a seat at a far off table, a table that my friends and I normally didn't sit at. "Eat," he commanded once I plopped down next to him.

I looked at my choices. Meat surprise, an apple, some sort of salad that looked more like macaroni than leafy greens and an alarming amount of French fries.

"Thanks." I took the apple from the tray and nibbled on a fry.

"About what I said…" His voice was low, almost impossible to hear. I scooted closer, not sure I wanted to hear him defend his behavior or pity me for the rumors flying around school about Demetri's cheating scandal.

"I was upset."

"I know." The fry in my finger felt soggy, I threw it onto the napkin and wiped my hands. "I was too."

Alec grabbed my hand and held it in his lap, rubbing his thumb delicately over the tender flesh on my wrist. "Will you forgive me?"

Not what I expected. I looked back at the soggy fries and bit my lip. "Alec, there wasn't ever anything to forgive. I was the one being insensitive."

His grip lessened on my hand.

"But..." I turned toward him and then shied away, I hadn't realized how close we were sitting until right then. Close enough to kiss him, for crying out loud! "You can't keep shutting me out and keeping me in the dark like this! I mean, some days I really like you, I lo—" I stopped myself as I felt my cheeks stain crimson. "I love hanging out with you. You're one of my best friends, and some days I feel like, I don't know... Like you are trying to push me away. And then all this stuff with Demetri trying to strip me naked and then in the same breath, talking cryptically about being the first. I don't know. I'm just really confused."

Alec's eyes flickered to my lips then back up to my eyes. "I know. It's just that..." His voice cracked. He pulled his hand away and shook his head as he looked out the windows of the cafeteria. "The minute I tell you, is the minute I say goodbye to you forever."

"You don't know that!" I grabbed his hand pleading with him to trust me, just once.

"Give me time to believe that, Nat." Alec smiled sadly and squeezed my hand. The lunch bell rang.

"Are you gonna follow me to my next class?"

Alec laughed. "Do you want me to?"

I blushed. "Kind of."

"Then yes, I'll follow you to class."

"Will you stay?"

"Do you want me to?"

"Are we really doing this right now?" I glared.

Alec picked up the trays and my messenger bag. "I'll take you, but I need to go to class too. I have a lot of learning to do."

"Clearly." I smirked.

As promised, he took me to Geology and went on his merry way toward his class, but not before turning around and giving me the most seductive wink in high school history. My knees went weak and suddenly I wasn't so sad about Demetri. My heart still clenched, but part of it was because I sensed he was hurting and I didn't know what I did to cause it or what I could do to fix it. Even though I wasn't completely certain of our relationship status, I still loved him. He was more than just a boyfriend. Demetri was a friend, someone I wouldn't wish to hurt in any way, though I knew I was probably doing exactly that every time I fell asleep dreaming of his brother, rather than of him.

I reached into my pocket and pulled out my phone and texted him again.

HOPE U R HVING A GD DAY. U SHD B PLEASED. ALEC MADE ME EAT. THE FRIES WR SOGGY. —NAT

Satisfied, I tucked my phone back into my front pocket and pretended to listen to my teacher.

Chapter Twenty-One

I had more homework than I thought possible. Weren't they supposed to lighten up after finals? It had been a week since Demetri and I'd had our fight or whatever that was. He still hadn't texted me back, and the media had been ruthless about Anjelica and their outings.

I was upset. But I had no right to be. Obviously we were over, but it still hurt. And yes, I had kissed his brother, and been guilty of loving him more than I should, but I had lost a friend, a good friend, and just looking at him on TV made me sad. He was supposed to be coming back in two days, and I wasn't sure I was ready to face him.

Alec and I hung out every night. We watched movies, played his stupid games, but he never touched me. Whatever had gone on between us was clearly over. He was back to his old respectable self, yet there were flickers of our past relationship. Sometimes when we ate popcorn and our fingers brushed, he would jerk back. I accidently fell asleep a few times during movies. It wasn't my fault his chest was more comfy than the couch. I hoped to God I didn't talk in my sleep because I almost always woke up sprawled across his lap.

"Nat, wake up." He would brush the hair across my face and then his hands would pull back as he waited for me to get up from the couch on my own and groggily walk back to my house. I shivered at the memories of the past week.

I shook my head and looked back at my homework. It was Friday and I wasn't in the mood. I decided to go to the beach and listen to music. I hadn't done that in a while and I felt more emotional than usual.

I put on a sweatshirt and ran out of the house. It took me five minutes to get to my favorite spot next to the tall grass that edged the white sand. The music soothed my nerves. Actually it soothed my fear and insecurity about everything going on with Alec and Demetri, but then again, music had a way of doing that. I took a deep breath and closed my eyes.

I must have fallen asleep because I woke up extremely chilled. My teeth chattered as I grasped the sweatshirt tighter around me.

"So are you attempting suicide or merely stupid?" A dark voice asked from behind me.

"Hello to you too, friend," I grumbled stretching my arms above my head as I stole a peek at Alec.

His lips slightly parted, his tongue slipped out to wet them and then he cursed and ran a hand through his hair. "I didn't know where you were."

"Well, you found me." I shivered again but didn't want to get up, call it stubbornness, but I wanted to stay put.

"I swear you're aging me, Nat," Alec mumbled as he took a seat next to me and pulled me into his embrace.

"Sorry?"

"Not much of an apology, but I'll take it." He moved his hand quickly over my shoulders and then began massaging my neck. I moaned and dipped my head forward as his fingers dug into my sore flesh.

We sat there, silent for a few minutes, other than my moaning. His touch felt so good. He hadn't touched me since the dance.

"Alec?"

"Hmm?"

I swallowed the fear and pressed forward. "Do you trust me yet?"

I heard his deep sigh so I kept my head down as he continued to massage. "Getting there, Nat. Getting there."

Nodding, I licked my lips and stuffed my hands in the pockets of my sweatshirt. "Okay."

"Do you have plans tonight?"

I laughed. "You mean besides my failed suicide attempt?"

His hand stilled and then he pulled me into a side hug and kissed my head. "Yes, besides that."

"Nope."

"Good." He jumped up, dusting the sand off of his torn jeans, and held out his hand. "Let's watch a movie."

"Deal."

We walked hand in hand back to the house. I moved around his kitchen, familiar with my surroundings, considering it had been like a second home to me, and made some popcorn.

Alec set up the movie then grabbed a few sodas and poured them over crushed ice. We settled onto the couch and he pressed play.

"Twilight?" I squeaked. "Really?"

He shrugged. "I'm trying to earn points."

"For being an ass half the time?" I countered.

"Of course not." Alec nudged me. "For being an ass at least three quarters of the time."

"Ah, that's sweet."

"Glad you agree." He winked and put his arm around me. It was the most he had touched me in days. I craved his nearness, so I very slowly curled up next to him and sighed, content to watch werewolves and vampires fight over a girl who had dead eyes.

Unfortunately, neither of us realized, that is until after the credits were rolling, how similar our story was.

Well, if you took out the whole I'm going to kill you in order to love you thing, it was basically the same.

A sordid love triangle with two very different boys who both refused to let me in on their secret.

"Probably a poor choice considering…" Alec's voice trailed off.

I nodded mutely.

"But I'm curious." Alec turned down the TV and twisted his body to face me. "Would I be more of a Jacob or an Edward?"

I put a hand over my mouth to stifle my laugh.

"Forget it." Alec cursed and made a move to get up.

"I'm sorry, no stay!" I laughed and tried to tug him back down to the couch and managed to get my giggles under control. "You have to understand that guys don't just go walking around asking things like that."

"I know." His clenched teeth and rigid posture told me all I needed to know. I sighed and leaned back in order to really take him in. His form was big, muscular. He was dark, dangerous, brooding, funny. He was everything. I let out a little gasp.

His eyes narrowed. "What?"

Embarrassment washed over me as I looked down at my clenched hands and whispered, "You're kind of both."

"As in a hybrid?" he asked.

I glanced up, he was grinning like an absolute fool. His smile did funny things to me. It made me feel like I wanted to attack him but hold his hand at the same time and enjoy the feel of his palm against mine. Smiles were a special case, and I sometimes wished he would reserve them only for me.

"Yes, Alec. A hybrid, you're like a vampwolf." I burst out laughing and turned away. He pounced on me, his body hovered over mine.

"Is my man card gone now?" His face was so close to mine I could only see his lips as they formed the words.

My eyes traced the corner of his firm jaw. "No." I reached up and trailed my hand down his muscular shoulder and arm.

He shuddered. "Damn it." His eyes flashed. For a second I was scared and then he was kissing me. With a groan my body flared to life as his muscular form covered mine. I was suffocating in him. I needed him so much it was painful. I reached for his shoulders and pulled him closer. He wedged his leg between mine then reached for my hips pulling me against him.

Alec had never kissed me like this. He placed his hands behind me and grasped my butt as he deepened the kiss. Frantic, I reached for his shirt. He was already there without my help. He tugged it off giving me an amazing view of his tattooed body and muscled abs. I gasped and gave an involuntary shudder.

"Nat, you drive me crazy."

"Good crazy?" I asked breathlessly as he gazed down at me.

He tilted my chin upward and kissed the corner of my mouth. "Crazy crazy."

"Oh."

"Yeah, *oh*." He chuckled against my neck, then began sucking below my ear before returning to my lips. I reached for the buttons of his jeans, but he pushed my hands back down, pinning me against the couch.

I tried again, but he pushed me away, this time slapping at my hands.

I laughed and let my hands fall to my side. "Seriously?"

He nuzzled my neck. "I'm not that kind of guy."

Sighing, I tilted my head to give him better access. "Right now, I kind of wish you were."

His hands stilled, his lips frozen on my neck. *Crap. What*

did I do?

"You can't say things like that to me, Nat. Not when we're like this, because I want nothing more than to take you on this couch and very aggressively, very slowly, very purposefully, have my way with you."

"Okay."

"Nat," he warned, his arms flexing as he braced himself above me.

I knew he was painfully turned on. I mean how could I not tell? But I was just as uncomfortable as he was. I wanted him. And it wasn't just my hormones speaking, it was so much deeper.

"I know what you're thinking," he said.

"No, you don't."

"But I do." He kissed my lips, softly tugging on the bottom one, then biting down causing a pleasurable pain. "You think it would be worth it, but I promise you, that's not the case."

"Why?"

"Because you don't know what kind of guy I am."

"But I do!"

His eyes got very sad as he bowed his head to touch mine. "Nat, you don't."

"Then tell me, and let me make my choice."

"What if by telling you, I lose you?"

"Do you really think I'm that kind of person?"

"Yes and no." He wrapped his hands around my head and pressed his mouth against mine, deepening the kiss, his tongue swirled in my mouth causing sensations to flare to life all throughout my body. He tasted so sweet, his body was so warm. I felt comfortable and scared all at once. Excited, yet cautious. Being with Alec was like trying to tame a tiger. You never knew if he was going to play fair or if he was going to pounce.

I pressed my palm flat against his chest and closed my

eyes as I allowed myself to get lost in his kiss. Soon I realized I was no longer in a situation I could control, but then again maybe I hadn't ever been in control. Not when it came to Alec. He groaned and lifted me then threw me back onto the couch so that he was straddling near my hips, his hands moved to my chest and then dipped under my shirt.

I should have realized that something would go wrong. After all, hadn't everything?

I didn't hear the door click.

Nor did I hear anyone shout our names.

By the time I opened my eyes it was too late. Demetri stood there, a sad smile on his lips. I nudged Alec, he pulled back and then scowled.

"Second again, brother. Don't you have a little starlet to go screw?"

I slapped him so hard my hand stung.

Tears streamed down my face as I struggled to get out from under his hold. Alec held me firm. I twisted in his grip. Nobody said a word. What. The. Hell.

Demetri didn't move. He watched me struggle. Watched his brother and shook his head before dropping his bag to the floor. "I came home early to see Nat."

"But…" Words failed me.

"I lost my phone," he said reading my mind. "Some Hollywood starlet was irritated that a nobody was texting me." He shifted his feet nervously and looked at the floor, his face slightly red.

Numb, I glared at Alec, willing him to say something, anything to make the pain in my chest go away.

Nothing. Absolutely nothing.

With a cry, I beat him with my fists until he relented, finally letting me escape from his hold. It was the second time in only five days that I had run crying from their house. Would I ever learn?

"Nat! Nat!" Alec screamed after me.

I pushed against the door to my house grunting with the impact.

Alec's arms braced around me holding me to him. "I'm sorry, Nat, I know how that appeared."

"Oh really, Alec?" I sobbed. "Because it looked pretty life-shattering."

His arms tensed even more around me. "I know, but it isn't what it looked like."

I hung my head. "So you didn't just make out with me in hopes that your brother, who apparently still is my boyfriend, would come home and catch us. You are a piece of work, you know that? Both of you! I hate both of you!" My voice cracked as my body slumped back against his.

"He's lying to you!" he shouted, making the hair on the back of my arms stand at attention.

"How do you even know that? He didn't have his phone."

"I just know him, Nat, okay?" His voice strained in the nighttime air. "Are you going to be alright?"

"No." I turned around in his arms, my face inches from his. "I'm not just going to be alright. You said he was second, suggesting that you got to me first. What the hell, Alec? You're not that guy. I don't believe it. Why would you hurt me like that? Why would you throw something like that in his face?"

"It doesn't matter."

"So I don't matter?"

Alec muffled a curse. "That's not what I said."

We stood in silence, me still in his arms, and Alec's breathing turning more ragged by the second. His head descended, and he very gently brushed a kiss across my lips. I was still in too much shock to push away. His words jolted me out of it.

"I was mad, okay? I know it was uncalled for. I'm sorry."

"Damn right, you're sorry!" I tried to pull away, but he tilted my chin up for another kiss. I couldn't think when he was near me, when he was kissing me as if I was his reason for living.

I threw my arms around his neck and opened my mouth to him, the kiss deepened, and my hunger for him grew. Even though I wanted to hate him, my heart wouldn't let me.

"What are you doing to me?" I whispered against his lips, finally allowing my body to fully slump into his embrace.

Alec nibbled my lower lip and pulled me into a tight hug. "Let me go talk to him for a minute, okay? Leave your window open tonight."

"So you can sneak in and have your way with me?" I glared.

Alec shook his head. "So I can pull you into my arms and tell you everything's going to be okay."

I shivered and crossed my arms over my chest while I watched him run back into his house. Part of me wanted to chase after him, to see what kind of fight he and Demetri would get into. I wanted to believe Demetri, but pictures didn't lie.

I walked into my house and flipped on the TV. Now would be a good time to have piles of chocolate conveniently placed in a bowl on the table, but we needed to go grocery shopping. There wasn't a morsel of chocolate in the house.

I settled for popcorn, crossed my legs and flipped to the entertainment channel.

Of course it wasn't long before Demetri's beautiful face popped on.

"Must be nice being a rock star!" the commentator gushed. "Demetri Daniels was seen leaving another club late last night with yet another starlet on his arm! This time he made his intentions known as he snuck a kiss briefly before going into another club. Our party boy must be tired. He was seen going back to his hotel at four A.M!"

I glared at the TV.

It wasn't what the reporter was saying that bothered me.

Nope, it was the picture of Demetri looking at his cell phone and then putting it into his pocket.

Lying bastard.

If he had it yesterday, he saw all my texts.

Irritated and way more hurt than I thought possible, I threw the remote onto the couch and marched up to my room, slamming the door in the process. I didn't even bother to wash my face. I tumbled under the covers and fought back tears. Why would he lie to me? Had he been lying the whole time? What purpose would that serve?

I hid further under the covers then remembered Alec wanted me to leave my window open, I hopped out of bed and opened the latch then tried desperately to fall asleep.

Chapter Twenty-Two

I awoke to Alec kissing me, which on one hand could be considered slightly horrifying. Since I hadn't washed any makeup off my face, I knew I looked slightly insane if not at least partially unstable.

I opened my eyes. His large body was hovering over mine. "Hey."

"Hey, yourself." I blinked my eyes so they could adjust to the pure male beauty in front of me and then Alec smiled. It was his same magic smile, the one he reserved only for me. I sighed.

After a few minutes of silence Alec spoke. "He's sorry."

"I don't care if he's sorry. Sorry means he realizes what he did was wrong. Sorry means he wasn't lying to me the entire time we were together. How the hell can you defend him?"

Alec cursed. "He's my brother. It's my job to protect him. Even if it's from himself. You don't understand. It's complicated."

"And me? What about me?" I tried to wriggle away from him, but his arms braced my shoulders as he leaned down and kissed my forehead.

"I'm pretty sure my only job from here on out is to show you how much I love you."

Damn him. Leave it to Alec to say the one thing that melted all my defenses and made me want to throw my body at him like some lovesick teenager. Then again if the shoe fit…

"Alec?" My voice cracked. "Was he lying the whole time?"

Cold air met me as Alec threw back the covers and joined me in my bed. "No, Nat. He really did care about you. I think in his own twisted way he thought he was doing us a favor."

"By being a bastard?"

"Come on, take his age into account, he's immature."

"He's a year younger than you," I pointed out. "Besides, how is him being a complete ass helping anyone?"

"It's com—"

"I swear if you say it's complicated one more time I'm going to throw you out the window."

Alec laughed and nuzzled my neck. "I'd like to see you try."

"You doubt me?"

His tongue blazed a trail down my neck. "Absolutely."

A moan escaped my lips before I could pretend to be totally indifferent to his kisses and his touch.

Alec pulled my body against his then dipped his hands behind my head pulling it so I was resting on his shoulder staring directly at his lips.

"Now what?" I whispered, still focused on the perfect shape of his jaw as his lips broke into a smile.

"I have my way with you?"

I rolled my eyes and pushed away enough to look up at his face. "You're so romantic. Really, you take my breath away. I almost swooned just now. Good thing I'm lying down."

Alec chuckled and brought my hand to his lips to kiss it.

"Fine, I won't have my way with you yet… but," he laced his fingers in between mine, "I'd really like to take you out on a date."

I wanted to date him. I wanted to do much more than that, but what would people say? I wasn't normally the type of girl that worried about stuff like that, but after all the media buzz around my and Demetri's relationship I knew it would blow up in my face if Alec and I were seen out and about.

"People are going to say I'm a whore."

"Don't." Alec's grip tightened on my hand as he pulled me closer to him. "This is my fault, not yours. I should have stayed away from you."

"I'm glad you didn't."

We stayed like that for what felt like an eternity, both of us searching the other's eyes, willing the other person to say something, to confess that it's been like this since our first meeting.

It wasn't ever just a pen that he picked up off the floor.

It was so much more. And though I tried to be with the guy that Alec kept pushing me toward, my heart wouldn't ever let go.

"Stupid pen," I grumbled.

"Huh?"

I giggled. "Never mind. So…" I played with the hair on the back of his head, twisting it between my fingers. "About this date."

"I'll do anything. Just don't stop." Alec rested his head against my chest and groaned.

"Our date?" I reminded him.

"Uh-huh." His hands wrapped around my body hugging me close to him as I continued to play with his hair and rub his neck. "I think I may like this better than sex."

I froze.

"Damn, did I say that out loud?" Alec tensed above me. I burst out laughing.

"At least I know what I need to do to get you to confess to me all your dirty little secrets."

"That's bribery and manipulation, a federal offense…" His words trailed off as he moaned again and relaxed against me.

"You were saying," I whispered as I wrapped my hands around the base of his neck then worked down to his broad shoulders.

"Marry me."

"No."

"Why?"

"Because you only asked so you'd have a personal masseuse."

"I have other reasons."

"I'm sure you do."

"Fine, but I'm asking again tomorrow," Alec grumbled and turned his head so his ear was pressed against my chest.

His admission should have scared me. I mean, he was kidding, but I knew Alec. He didn't really kid about stuff. He was the serious one, the brooding one, the one who made girls want to pass out when he crooned into the microphone. I shivered.

"You cold?"

Nope, just hot for you and pretty freaked out that you just joked about marrying me. "I'm good."

"Nat."

"Hmm?"

"I love you."

Holy crap. I froze again. It felt like my heart stopped beating, but I knew I was alive because I was still breathing. He really needed to stop surprising me like that. I mean, I'm young, but a girl can only handle so much.

I took an earth-shattering breath. The type that you need before you say something that you know is going to shift the planes of your universe, the type you take when it's inevitable that nothing in your life is ever going to be the same.

"I love you, too."

****

I got into the backseat of Alec's SUV and began nervously wringing my hands together. I knew Demetri would be riding with us. I also knew Demetri probably noticed that Alec didn't sneak back into their house until about an hour ago. It didn't help that he had a very satisfied grin on his face.

I took special care in dressing plain. I didn't want anyone staring at me, I wanted no attention whatsoever. To get attention meant people would notice the not so subtle looks Alec threw my way.

Demetri emerged from the house. He opened the car door and glanced at me. "Hey, Nat." His voice was sad. I wanted to reach out and touch him, but the temptation to strangle him was also really strong, so I kept my hands in my lap and nodded.

"Hey, Demetri."

"Listen—" Demetri turned around while Alec drove the car out of the driveway. Oh gosh, there wasn't any escape at all. I had to sit there and look into Demetri's eyes while he made me feel like a complete jerk, when really he was the one who was whoring around. Not that I was any better. I cringed when I thought of my behavior over the past few weeks.

"I'm sorry."

"Huh?" I felt my jaw drop.

He shrugged. "I'm sorry I lied." And that was it. He turned back around. No more apologies, no more words. It was as if the past few months didn't even happen. Our history together, the drama between the two of them. I mean, didn't I at least get an explanation?

The rest of the ride to school was filled with awkward silence and the sound of my breathing. At least that's what it felt like. By the time Demetri hopped out of the car and I opened my door, I wanted to turn right back around and jog home.

"Hey..." Alec grabbed me as I sat on the edge of the seat, my legs hanging out the door. "If it makes you feel better, it's rare for him to admit he's wrong about anything."

I nodded. "Okay,"

"Class?" Alec held out his hand. I grabbed it. Yes, people would talk and they would stare, but I needed his strength to get me through the day.

By the time the lunch bell rang I was actually feeling pretty positive about the whole situation. Nobody had said anything about my and Demetri's very public break up, and even though I noticed some girls whispered when I walked in with Alec, for the most part it was a normal day in Hell.

"Nat!" Evan waved me over to our usual table. "So," he said when I took a seat. "You cut off his balls?"

"Evan!" I slapped him and felt my cheeks blush crimson. "It's not as bad as that. I mean, he's a rock star. It's not my business if that's the circle he wants to date in."

"Huh?" Evan looked between me and Alec then leaned forward. "Not talking about last night's news, Nat. I'm talking about today's."

"Today's?" I looked to Alec, but his eyes were already trained on something across the room. His jaw clenched. I followed his eyes and gasped.

Demetri was making out with a girl from my class. His hands everywhere on her body. I gripped the chair and called him every name I could possibly think of in my head.

Alec made a move to get up. I reached out and stopped him. "Just let him, Alec. If this is how he wants to deal with the past few months, then let him."

Alec did not look convinced. In fact, it looked like he wanted to murder someone. He pulled out his cell and in very clipped, scary tones ordered one of the security team to give

Demetri aid. Like that was going to help, what was he going to do, castrate him?

Sure enough, Bob moved very swiftly through the gathering crowds and whispered something in Demetri's ear as he assaulted the girl in his chair.

He leaned back, just enough to make eye contact with me, and then with his eyes opened kissed the girl again, alternating between licking her face and tugging her lower lip.

It was like watching porn.

If porn took place in high school.

And the lead was a rock star.

"Sometimes I hate my brother." Alec cursed. "Now do you wonder why we need to take a year off touring? Clearly we've got issues."

"We?" I lifted my eyebrow.

"Yeah, *we*." Alec looked down and cursed again.

Within minutes Demetri's little show was over, and wonder of all wonders as he walked away from the girl who was now pouting in the corner, he grabbed another. Yes, another girl, and began to kiss her.

What type of girl kisses another guy when they still have remnants of a previous kiss plastered across their face?

She pulled back after a few minutes. And I watched Demetri stagger behind Bob as he was escorted out of the cafeteria.

"Is he drunk?"

Alec was silent.

"Alec?"

"Probably." He looked away. "He doesn't handle rejection well."

"He did this!" I pointed at the door, angry that Alec would again take the blame for choices someone else was making. "Not us!"

Alec looked like he wanted to scream; he shook his head and then ran his fingers through his hair. "I know, Nat. It's just hard to watch this again."

"What are you talking about?"

"I'll tell you, just not now."

I nodded, but didn't trust his word. Both guys had been ridiculously secretive about whatever incident happened between them two years ago. It was stupid vain hope that kept me trusting that he would keep to his promise and actually say something.

The bell rang. "Come on, I'll walk you to class." He threw my bag over his shoulder and grabbed my hand.

The rest of the day went by smoothly. Two girls asked me if I was dating the other brother in AD2 now that Demetri was clearly occupied. I glared, and briefly contemplated giving them the finger.

Needing to calm my temper. I stomped over to my locker and threw my books inside. Escape… I needed to escape before I said something that would make me more of a target.

I pushed through the front doors of my school, a hand reached out and jerked me back just as my feet touched the curb.

It was Demetri.

"Nat," he groaned, pulling me against him, his head dipping down as if he wanted to kiss me. He smelled like whiskey, I pushed away from him but he held me fast. "Nat, I didn't mean it."

"Demetri, stop, you're drunk." Frantic, I looked around for Alec, but he wasn't anywhere near us. Kids continued to trickle out of the school. *Please hurry, Alec.*

"I'm not that drunk." He swayed on his feet. Really? He was completely and totally wasted. "I just need to talk to you I just want to tell you why!"

Okay, no shouting. I patted him on the arm. "Okay, why?"

"I love you."

Oh no.

"I love you so much and I know you love him! I know

you do! I saw you two, the way you looked at each other! I didn't want to be second." Here we go again with this second crap.

"Listen, Demetri. You really need to get your crap together. I'm sorry we didn't work out. I'm also sorry that you didn't have the balls to say it to my face before you stormed out and hooked up with the first girl in L.A. you could find."

"We didn't." He looked down and shoved his hands in his pockets. "We didn't hook up, I kept thinking about you. Saw your texts." He swayed again then braced himself against the brick wall backing me up against it.

"I saw them, Nat. I wanted to respond so bad, but I needed time to think. And then Alec does what he does best."

"What's that?"

"Steals the only girl I love."

"Oh, so he makes a habit of that?" I sneered, angry that he would again blame Alec for his obvious poor choices.

"You have no idea how messed up we are."

"I'm beginning to understand," I answered, teeth clenched.

"He stole her."

"Okay, Demetri." I patted him on the arm and stepped around him.

He reached out and tugged me against him. "No, you don't understand. My girlfriend. He slept with her, got her pregnant, abandoned her."

Nausea rolled over me. "He said it was a one night stand."

"With my girlfriend." Demetri scowled. "Who was too much of a good girl to even think about sleeping with me. She slept with him."

I gulped. I wanted to throw my hands over my ears and tell him to stop talking, that I couldn't listen anymore, but I was frozen, unable to move as he stepped closer and continued.

"She was mine!" Demetri's voice cracked. "And he knew it! He was such a cocky son of a bitch. We were drunk. He said I needed to seal the deal. I told him it was impossible, so we made a bet."

I didn't like where this was going.

"He said if he got into her pants that I owed him a new car." Demetri looked away from me, tears blurring his large blue eyes. "I laughed it off. Alec was always the player. I knew he'd try, but she loved me. I knew she loved me. Just like I knew you loved me. And now…" Demetri cursed and punched the wall with his fist, blood trickled down his knuckles. "Now she's dead."

The wall where we stood began to spin. I tried to balance myself, tried to lean on Demetri but he had already walked off, leaving splatters of blood in his wake. I fell to my knees.

"Nat!" Alec called my name, but it hurt too much to breathe let alone speak. "Nat!"

I swallowed, air whooshed by my ears. My eyes began to feel heavy as tunnel vision took over.

"Nat!" His voice was closer, and then I was moving through the air. "Damn it, Nat. Don't you dare pass out on me!" Alec's hand was warm against my face. My eyes flickered and then focused on him.

He half-carried me, half-walked me to his SUV and helped me inside. Too shocked to say anything, all I could do was stare at the heating vents in front of me. The slam of the car door jolted me back from my current state. I looked at Alec and gasped.

Blood trickled from his lip.

"You lose a fight?" I asked weakly.

"Not funny." Alec hit his hands against the steering wheel. "You scared the crap out of me, Nat! Are you okay? Did you eat today?"

I looked down at my trembling hands. "No."

He cursed again and pulled out of the parking lot. I tried

to sit up to buckle my seatbelt, but by the time I fumbled with the lock, he had already driven into the McDonald's driveway.

He ordered me fries, ice cream, and a Coke.

"Sugar, salt, carbs, and caffeine." Alec parked in a nearby lot and turned off the car. He pushed the food towards me and nearly growled when he said, "Eat. Now."

"No."

"Nat, I'm not in the mood to argue with you."

"And I'm not in the mood to hear about your entire sordid history with Demetri, but that's what happened about fifteen minutes ago!"

Alec's eyes widened, he looked away and didn't say anything for a very long time.

"He told you everything."

I nodded even though he wasn't looking at me. "Tell me it isn't' true."

Alec laughed bitterly. "I can't do that."

"Can't or won't?"

After a heavy sigh, Alec looked at me his eyes full of sadness. "I can't deny the truth. I did everything he said, and what's probably worse is I got her hooked on drugs in the process."

I closed my eyes.

"Nat…" His voice was a whisper.

"Just take me home."

We rode home in silence. My brain tried to put together the pieces of the puzzle. Alec had single-handedly destroyed a woman's life, all because of his cocky attitude and rock star ways. He hurt his brother so much that I'm surprised they still spoke to one another. And now it all made sense.

Being first and second.

The way they had switched roles.

Demetri dealt with pain the way Alec had originally dealt with life. Drink, have sex, and numb yourself to everything around you. Alec shied away, like a turtle in a shell, continuing to punish himself for the crappy decisions he made.

When the car pulled up to my house I didn't move.

"Nat…"

I closed my eyes, unable to believe I was about to utter the words that I was thinking. "Tell me everything."

"It's complicated. I don't think..."

"Tell me. Now."

Chapter Twenty-Three

Alec's story was worse than Demetri's account. The only difference was what he had already admitted to. He was a cocky piece of work and was pissed at his brother for messing up a huge deal for them with a new TV show that was supposed to document their entire tour.

He was also, as he admitted, jealous that Demetri had a girl who loved him so completely, so when Demetri made the bet out of humor, Alec took him seriously.

"Heroin." He laughed humorlessly. "I told her it would help her relax." Alec refused to look at me. "We had been partying all weekend and Demetri was already in bed. She was drunk."

I wiped some stray tears from my eyes. And kept listening.

"It was all over within twenty minutes. Neither of us was really thinking. Had I been thinking, I wouldn't have gone through with it. But alcohol? Drugs? They have a way of messing with you. I knew what I was doing, I just didn't care. I knew it was wrong, but I felt so good — it felt so good — that I refused to acknowledge there would be any consequences."

He cursed and shook his head. "Demetri found us in bed together."

My heart was in my throat.

"I've never seen that look on his face before. They had a huge fight, broke up, and we didn't hear from her again until we found out she was pregnant. By then we also found out she was hooked on everything under the sun, made easy by yours truly, considering I paid her off to keep her mouth shut."

We sent her into rehab. Our little boy, whom I never met, went to his grandma's. The next we heard from her, she was released from rehab and sounded really happy. I apologized again and told her how sorry I was. She and Demetri talked on the phone and got in a fight. She, um… She went to pick up Benjamin and was hit in a head on collision. She went the wrong way on the freeway."

I closed my eyes and spoke, my voice hoarse from trying to keep my emotions in check. "So the canceled concert tour this year? The time off?"

"Grief counseling and addiction."

"Addiction?"

"Not me, Nat." Alec bit his lip. "I don't touch the stuff. I don't touch anything. It ruined a part of me that I don't think I'll ever get back. The addiction? That would be my brother's. Also my fault."

"He makes his own choices. It's not your fault." I had no idea why I was defending him.

He laughed bitterly. "Yeah, I think it is, Nat. It was all me. I was the partier, the wild one. I never got in trouble, I never had any consequences. Somehow, I got lucky, and for some reason I never felt addicted. I just liked the feeling drugs gave me. That was not the case with Demetri."

"Is he on drugs now?"

"I don't know." Alec shrugged. "He's drinking heavily again, that much is clear. Nat…" He turned to me. "You don't have to stay. You can go." His eyes watered. "I kill everything

I touch. It's like I'm poison."

"No!" I reached for him but he jerked back. I reached for him again and pulled him into my arms, the console kept us from being closer, but I needed to reassure him. I needed him to know that I was there for him.

"Alec, look at me." His gaze fluttered to mine. "What you did was messed up. I'm not going to deny it. Nor am I going to say that I'm not seriously tempted to jump out of this car and run away from you, but I love you. I love who you are now. The man you are now. If those things wouldn't have happened to you, who knows where you would be?"

Alec trembled in my arms his body tight with tension. "Nat, you have to know. I'm not that guy anymore. I don't even know who that guy was, I just—"

My kiss was forceful and pleading. I wrapped my hands around his shoulders, jerking him closer to me. His tongue licked my lower lip then dove into my mouth instantly driving me insane. Never had I been kissed so desperately. My body was on fire for him. I needed to be closer. Part of me believed that if I just showed him, rather than used my words, how I felt, he would begin to understand the depth of my feelings.

"Nat—" Alec groaned against my mouth, his hands gripping my shoulders as he pushed me tenderly away. "I love you so much, you know that right? I would never do anything to hurt you."

"I know."

Rain began to fall, sounding like a loud applause. I smiled, and grabbed my backpack. "Race you to the house?"

Alec's jaw seemed to relax in relief, his smile warmed me. "Yeah, Nat, race you to the house."

I beat him, mainly because I cheated. I was closest to the door, and it's possible that I threw my bag at him in order to make it there in time.

Alec laughed. He was drenched from head to toe. His plain grey t-shirt plastered against his body. Suddenly it was extremely difficult to breathe as I watched his chest rise and fall. My eyes drifted shut as he reached out and traced my face with his hand. "You're so beautiful, Nat."

Not compared to him. He was a god among teenagers, and he was all mine. I rose to my tiptoes expectantly. He chuckled and lifted me off the ground for a kiss and crushed his lips to mine.

I wanted so many things. To sigh, to laugh, to tell him to never let me go. But our moment was interrupted when the door was thrown open.

"Get a room or something," Demetri grumbled pushing past us, he wasn't even walking in a straight line.

Alec cursed. "Where the hell do you think you're going?"

"Out!" Demetri stumbled to his car and threw open the door. The wind picked up, whipping it across my face. My teeth began to clatter.

"The hell you are!" Alec ran toward the car and tried to jerk the door open, but Demetri locked the doors and slammed the car into drive. "Demetri! Don't!" Alec yelled until his voice was hoarse.

The Mercedes peeled out of the driveway and took off, almost hitting a few mailboxes on the way.

"Damnit!" Alec kicked the ground then ran to the side of his car and quickly jumped in. "Get in, Nat."

I did as I was told, still stunned that Demetri would be that stupid to get behind a wheel when he was wasted.

We followed in a tense silence, looking down the streets for any sign of Demetri. I didn't want to try his phone. The last thing we needed was for him to answer it while driving and hit something.

I heard the sirens first.

Alec was still busy cursing to himself and blaming himself for every little thing on the planet.

I prayed I was wrong.

But that same feeling that overtook me on the first day of

school - the one that made me wonder if life was ever going to be the same - washed over me. The hair raised on the back of my arms. I closed my eyes and prayed, prayed that I was wrong. Prayed that Demetri was okay.

We turned the corner.

And I saw his car.

He had taken the corner too fast and gone straight into an abandoned building. I could only see the taillights of the crushed car.

Within minutes we heard sirens. I choked back a sob. "Alec, pull over!"

"I can't, Nat! I have to find Demetri, I have to—" The words died on his lips as he glanced at the accident ahead of us.

"No." He shook his head while he pulled into the spot across the street. "No." He slammed the car door and ran outside. My eyes filled with tears. I ran out of the car and grabbed my phone. Alec was yelling at the cops, the paramedics, everyone.

"Mom?" I yelled when she answered. "Mom! It's Demetri! He's been in an accident! I'm here. I'm safe, yes. Mom, the ambulance is here. Oh, Mom, I don't know what to do." I sobbed into the phone. "Mom, I need you now!"

The phone clicked off. Within minutes my mom had her arms around me pulling me into a tight embrace. The paramedics emerged from the building with Demetri lying across a stretcher.

Blood was everywhere.

Alec was shouting.

I wanted to fall to the ground, but I knew Alec needed me. I had to be strong. My mom walked me over to him, without thinking we both pulled him into a tight hug. And cried. All three of us.

"Are you his brother?" a man asked.

"Yes." I answered for Alec. He seemed to be in shock still.

"If you're riding with us, we need to go now." He jumped into the ambulance. Alec looked at me.

"Go!" I pushed him towards the doors. "We'll follow."

He nodded, seeming almost relieved that I made the decision for him.

Alec jumped into the ambulance. I reached for his hand and grabbed the keys out of it then ran back to his SUV.

My mom wordlessly got into her car. We both followed the ambulance the few miles it was to the hospital.

I was too numb to even know what I was doing. I mechanically parked as close as possible, then jumped out and ran as fast as I could toward the emergency room. My mom was close behind, but she was prattling into her phone.

The minute the doors opened I figured out why.

Dad was standing with his cell phone in his hand. He was in normal clothes again, meaning he was on his way home.

"Dad, you have to—" I fell into his arms.

"Nat." He hugged me tight. "He's going to be fine. I'm going in right now."

"Don't let him die, just don't let him…" I fell to the ground. My mom was behind me, trying to pull me into her arms. The last thing I saw when I looked up was my dad's disappearing form as he ran into the emergency room.

"Nat?" Alec's voice cracked behind me.

My mom helped me to my feet. But I was only up for a second before Alec pulled me into his arms. His body tense with exhaustion and worry. I rubbed his back. I knew I needed to be strong. As much as I was blaming myself for Demetri's actions, I knew Alec was taking it harder. He always did. It was like he lived with guilt over every bad choice Demetri made.

It felt like one of the horrible nightmares I had been having. Only, I wasn't the one hit with the car, nor was I the one in the accident. Exhausted, I fell against Alec. His strong hands came around my stomach, pulling me into a backward hug. My eyes darted to my mom who was speaking to one of the triage nurses.

I felt Alec sigh behind me. "We should go sit down."

My throat felt all closed up. I wasn't sure I could trust myself to speak without breaking down.

We sat in silence for over an hour and still hadn't heard anything. My grip on Alec's hand hadn't lessened any. I wasn't even sure he knew I was still sitting next to him. His eyes were trained on the double doors leading into the emergency room.

"He's going to be okay," I finally said, my hand clenching even tighter than before.

Alec said nothing. He didn't even blink.

I let go of his hand and began rubbing the back of his neck, desperate for him to make any sort of noise, or at least acknowledge that I was there. I didn't want him to feel alone.

"Alec," I tried again. "Is there anyone I need to call?"

Slowly, Alec shook his head. "I don't know, I can't think right now…"

"Your manager? Agent? Someone to handle the media?"

"Crap." Alec finally broke his stare from the double doors and looked at me. "Nat, I don't think I can do it, I can't—" His voice cracked.

"Give me your phone." I held out my hand.

Alec dug into his pocket and gave me his sleek silver iPhone, typing in the password before he gave it to me.

I scrolled through the address book. Alec was still tense next to me, but he watched me and then pointed out his agent's number.

I nodded and dialed.

Explaining the accident was earth-shaking. I didn't want to talk about it, but I was doing this for both Alec and Demetri. I repeated the story over twelve times to their managers, assistants, agents. Over an hour later I was finally hanging up and Alec's phone was blinking that it only had 20% battery power left.

My head pounded with the start of a headache as I shoved the phone back into his hand. "Thank you," he murmured.

I embraced him tightly and laid my head over his shoulder. "Any word?"

He shook his head. "Nothing."

"Is there anything else I can do?" I asked in a small voice.

Alec relaxed a bit and flashed me a small smile. "Honestly, Nat. You've gone above and beyond the call of duty. Just sit by me. It helps."

"I love you."

He was silent.

Dread filled my belly as I waited for his response. Did this change things between us? Did he blame me for Demetri's freak out?

"I love you too, Nat." His voice was hoarse.

Tears pooled in my eyes, and then the double doors flew open. My dad strode towards us, his eyes were tired. I could see the strain on his face.

It seemed like time stood still. Each step he took toward us felt like an eternity. I realized if I just concentrated on the floor where he was stepping, listened to the steady cadence of his shoes against the tile, I wouldn't pass out. I could even my breathing.

"Alec." My dad. The very same dad who hadn't once hugged me in my whole life, pulled my boyfriend into the tightest hug I've ever seen, and then opened his arms to me.

We stayed like that for a few minutes. Dad stepped back. "He's going to be fine."

I lost it.

Tears streamed down my face, my body wracked with sobs. Alec wordlessly pulled me to his side. "Can we see him?"

"Not yet." My dad looked from Alec to me. "We had to induce a coma so he could heal. We'll pull him out of it when I think he's out of the woods. He has four broken ribs, and a bruised spleen. His left wrist is completely shattered and one of his lungs was punctured. He has a mild concussion, and his face is severely bruised. His right cheek bone is fractured but other than that he's doing just fine."

Yeah, other than his entire body being broken. I could feel Alec tense next to me. I knew what he was thinking. His brother was okay, but he could have died. He's also left-handed, meaning he wouldn't be able to play guitar for quite a while. I knew enough about Demetri to know music was his only escape. I shuddered to think of what he would turn to if he didn't have his music.

"Sir?" Alec's voice cracked. "Thank you. I don't know what to say. Other than I owe you everything."

My dad smiled genuinely and patted Alec on the back. "It was my pleasure. Now, if you'll excuse me, I'm going to go check on our patient."

Guilt stabbed my chest. I had always thought my parents didn't care. Was it possible that they actually did? For my dad to do what he did, to embrace me, and then be so genuine with Alec. Confused, I just kept my mouth shut and allowed my brain to replay images of my past.

"Nat," Alec whispered next to me. My head snapped up. "Thank you, for taking care of things, for the calls and—" He shook his head and licked his lips then looked back down at the floor. "I honestly don't know what I would do without you."

I hugged him tight. "I'm sorry, Alec. If I could have known, maybe—"

"No." Alec jerked back and glared. "Don't even think about blaming yourself for this! We all go through crap, Nat. That's life. It's how you react to it that defines the person you grow into."

"Wise words from a nineteen year old. I wonder if you listen to your own advice?"

Alec cursed. "My situation is different, believe me. What I did, it was unforgiveable. I'm lucky my brother still talks to me."

"It's not different."

"The hell it isn't!" He yelled, his eyes widening, his mouth tense.

"Fine." I snapped. "How is it different? How is what you did any different?"

"I caused this!" Alec bolted from his seat and began pacing in front of me. "Do you even know the type of guy Demetri was before all this? Innocent little virgin who wouldn't even touch alcohol if someone paid him to! I protected him from everything and—"

Alec stopped talking.

"You sheltered him so much that he never learned how to deal with stuff on his own," I said. I knew Alec would be mad that I was butting in, but it was the truth. "Alec—" I got up and walked toward him. "You were the older brother. Yes, it was your job to protect him. But…" I shrugged. "Sometimes you gotta let people take the hit. How do you think a quarterback learns how to deal with the fear of getting hit?"

Alec snorted and looked away. "He gets the crap beat out of him at practice."

"Exactly." I reached up and brushed the hair away from his forehead. "Alec, you tried to protect Demetri from everything, and the minute things took a turn for the worse, how did he cope with it?"

"He didn't."

I kept talking. "So, then you tried harder, you changed your whole life, you coddled him even more, removed him from your old lifestyle, put him in counseling, tried to fix him, and then something else happened, and what was his reaction?"

Alec sighed. "The same as before, only this time he nearly killed himself."

"Alright then." I wrapped my hands around his head, pulling it down closer to mine. "I know I'm not perfect and we both know you aren't."

That got a laugh out of him.

"But, Demetri needs to grow up. He needs to learn, and hopefully this will be the start of that." I decided not to add in the part that Demetri was most likely facing criminal charges and would probably have to spend time in court over this escapade, nor the thought that he may not wake up at all. It hurt too much to think about.

Alec sighed. "You're right."

"I'm what?"

Glaring, Alec pushed me away with a laugh. "Don't push it, Nat."

"Alec?" A small nurse approached. "You can see your brother now. He's in ICU, but he's stable. I'm sure the doctor has informed you that he's in a medically induced coma, but you can still talk to him."

Alec clenched my hand.

"Sorry." The nurse looked between us. "Family only."

"She is family."

The nurse didn't looked convinced. Alec cleared his throat. "She's my *fiancée*."

Had I been any more alert I may have given away his little fib by gasping, but I was too tired to react. Instead I smiled and laid my head on his shoulder.

The nurse nodded. "Okay, this way."

Chapter Twenty-Four

I fought back tears as we walked into Demetri's room. A tube was coming out of his mouth, his face was bruised and bandaged. I choked back a sob when Alec fell to his knees next to his brother's bed. I didn't know what to say. What do you say? All of us were hurting, all in different ways. I did all I knew I could do. I put my hand on Alec's shoulder and watched a man, a very strong man, cry silently as he looked at his only remaining family, in a coma, in a hospital bed.

My fault, is all that ran through my head. The treacherous thoughts screamed at me! *Why did I go for Demetri when I knew my heart belonged to Alec? Why did I drag both of them through this?* I loved them both, I truly did. I was never one to understand people when they asked if you could love two people at one time. I thought they were stupid and selfish to even think of such a thing. But my heart was broken for the boy in the bed in front of me. I wanted to take his place. I wanted to remove the bandages one by one and kiss the bruises away.

My knees felt weak, so I walked over to the nearest chair and sat down. Alec didn't move. He grabbed his brother's hand. "I'm so sorry," he croaked.

The nurse came back in and told us it was time to leave.

I thought it would take ten men to get Alec to leave his brother's side, but he nodded his head and put his arm around me as we walked out.

"You need food," I said once we got back to the lobby. It had been hours since we had eaten.

"I never thought I'd see the day when you would be force feeding me," Alec joked. Tension released in my shoulders.

"Let's go grab some overnight stuff and some food and we can come back here."

"You sure you want to stay the night at the hospital?"

I exhaled. "I'm family, remember?"

"I won't ever forget." Alec kissed my cheek and we walked outside hand in hand.

****

The next three days flew by. I refused to go to school even though Alec was irritated with me for staying at the hospital. I couldn't leave Demetri's side any more than he could.

Like he said, we were family. I felt like I was the only family they had. It was like another half of my self was in that hospital bed.

Each night I would go into Demetri's room while Alec made phone calls to update his agent as well as his publicist. I was probably boring the poor guy to tears, but I kept reading from our senior lit class textbook as if nothing had happened. I'm sure inside Demetri was screaming for me to stop, which actually cheered me up when I got to the end of *Hamlet*.

The media had a field day with the accident. Some stations reported some really awful things, saying that Demetri had a drug problem, that he was high when he got into the accident. I was so angry most the time that when I walked out of the hospital and got a camera shoved in my face all I wanted to do was cry and lash out. Thankfully, Bob and Lloyd were lifesavers when it came to our security at the hospital. On several occasions I told them I wouldn't be upset at all if they suddenly lost control of their firearms.

They laughed.

Alec was talking quietly in the hall. I reached out and caressed Demetri's hand. His doctors had been slowly lessening the chemicals in his body. They figured he would be completely out his induced state over the next twenty-four hours. The bruises still looked dark and swollen across his face, but at least his lips had lost some of the swelling.

"Your brother told everyone I was his *fiancée*." I caressed his hand. "It was the only way they would let me see you." My chest clenched, I was too sad to laugh but I wanted to. "Trust me, I could have taken that tiny nurse. We all know how strong I am." I bit my lip and watched Demetri lay completely still, making no movement. "Alec also told me that you used to pee the bed when you were little and that you were scared of birds until you reached the age of twelve."

I laughed again and squeezed his hand. "Naturally, I thought the best way to get you out of your drug-induced state was to threaten you. So, I rented the movie *The Birds*, and if you don't come out of your coma I'm just going to keep playing it over and over again until you wake up."

"Cruel," Alec said behind me.

"And in order to prove my theory, I also recorded a few bird calls on my iPhone. Did you know there was an app for that?"

I could feel Alec's chuckle behind me as I pressed play. We both laughed, and then Demetri's hand moved.

I thought I imagined it, but Alec's hand froze on my shoulder. "Play it again."

I pressed play again, this time it was a crow, and yes, it was beyond creepy. My eyes trained on Demetri's hand.

Nothing.

Frustrated, I pushed the play button again. His hand moved, just slightly. I raised my gaze to his face.

"His eyes are open! Get the nurse!" I yelled. Alec was already out the door yelling down the halls.

Demetri's eyes widened as he looked around the room, his eyes filled with tears. "No, no, it's okay." I grabbed his hand and squeezed it. "You're fine, okay? Don't panic. I need you to not panic right now, okay?" I felt warm tears slide down my cheeks.

Demetri didn't nod, but his heart-rate went back to normal. I couldn't blame him. If I was strapped to equipment I would be freaking out too. They had removed his breathing tube earlier that morning, but I knew from my dad's stories that Demetri would have a severely sore throat for at least a week.

"Ice?" I reached for a cup of ice that I had set there in hopes that he would wake up soon. He nodded his head just slightly. I scooted closer and lifted the spoon to his chapped lips with trembling hands.

He opened his mouth just slightly, that same mouth I had spent endless days and hours kissing. I choked back another sob as he tried to smile and nod again. He liked it. He wanted more.

I giggled, and lifted more to his mouth.

"Well, well, well, it seems my daughter's treating our patient well." My dad had been my lifesaver these past few days, always answering questions and telling me that everything would be fine. I got choked up just thinking about it.

He walked to the monitors and wrote some stuff down on his clipboard, then began a slow examination of Demetri. "How are you feeling? Blink once if you are in pain, twice if you are okay for now."

Demetri blinked twice. I squeezed his hand in

encouragement.

"You've been in an accident," my dad stated. Demetri rolled his eyes as if to say no crap.

We all laughed nervously. Alec put his hand on my shoulder. I had one hand holding Demetri's and the other holding Alec's. I was the link between them, and it felt oddly right to be in the position I was in.

"You should have died," my dad said. Sheesh. Talk about no bedside manner. "I going to be honest with you, and I'm not going to sugar coat anything, son."

I saw a tear pool at the corner of Demetri's eyes. I wasn't sure if it was fear getting to him or the fact that my dad just called him "son", a term he hadn't heard for over ten years. Maybe it was a little bit of both.

"You have a long road ahead of you," my dad said. "I've made a few calls to enroll you in a local rehab program. The missus thinks it will be a good idea."

Demetri's eyes continued to pool with tears but in that moment he seemed strong, not weak. He stared at my dad as if he was some sort of god. "You're better than this, Son."

Okay, now I was getting choked up.

My dad sat on the bed and sighed. "You were made for more than music, more than just living on the edge, Son. I need you to believe that. I need you to work with me so we can get past this. Together. Can you do that?"

Tears streamed down my face as I watched Demetri slowly reach for my dad's hand and grasp it between his.

I wiped the tears away before my dad turned around, but his sixth sense picked it up anyway. He pulled me into a tight bear hug. "He's going to be fine, Baby. I'm going to leave you guys for a minute. I'll send the nurses in to start taking away some of that equipment hooked up to him."

I nodded and looked back at Demetri. His face was cracked into a half smile. "What are you smiling about?" I grinned.

His head moved slowly from side to side.

Alec laughed behind me and gently brought my back against him as he wrapped his arms around me. "I'm thinking it's the first time an adult has scolded him in years."

Demetri's smile widened.

We all laughed. I walked over to Demetri and kissed him on the forehead. "I love you, Demetri. I'll always love you." I grabbed his hand and placed it on my heart "You're right here. Always."

His eyes pooled with tears again, he nodded.

I walked out of the room, leaving the brothers alone with one another. It was time for me to go home and get some sleep. I found my dad at the nurse's station.

"Dad?" I was turning into an emotional basket case. He turned around, concern in his eyes. "I just needed to tell you…" Okay, insert hormonal teenager here. Tears streamed down my face. "Thank you, and I'm sorry. I love you so much. I'm so sorry."

"Baby girl." Within seconds I was in his arms. He was cradling my head in his hands and kissing my hair. "Oh, Baby. I'm the one who's sorry. Your mom said you two talked. I had no idea, Baby. I thought you were just going through a stage. I thought you wanted to be alone. But know this—" He pulled away from me, his eyes filled with tears. "You are my little girl. I love you so much. I would do anything for you. You are mine. Do you understand, Natalee? You are my flesh and blood and there is nothing on this Earth that is more important to me."

I half-expected the people around us to start clapping. His speech was beautiful, but not as beautiful as I felt in that moment.

For the first time in my life, I felt truly beautiful, and it was all because my father, my flesh and blood claimed me as his. I knew to whom I belonged, and his name was Paul Murray, my father."

I don't think I've ever cried so much in my life. I cried the whole way home. I cried as I made my way up the stairs, and when my mom burst into my room I cried again.

She held me, as all good moms should when their daughter is having an emotional breakdown. She promised we would try harder as a family, that we would work harder. She even asked for my forgiveness. And all because I fell in love with two boys.

I laughed through the last of the tears and changed into my sweats. I was exhausted. Tomorrow was Saturday. If all went well, I wanted to be rested up enough to visit Demetri without sobbing my eyes out or looking like a train had hit me.

Chapter Twenty-Five

I threw on a pair of sweats the following Sunday night and ran across the lawn to the guys' house. I knocked and waited.

Within seconds Alec appeared. Demetri's voice was yelling in the background, "Since when does she knock?"

Alec rolled his eyes and tugged me in for a heart-stopping kiss. I parted my lips. Things were just getting interesting, when we heard Demetri gagging from the living room.

Alec winked and stepped back. I laughed and followed him into the house.

Demetri had only been home for a few hours. It looked like a tornado had attacked their living room. Clothes and medicine were everywhere.

"Moving?" I asked as I noted the suitcases in the corner. The room went quiet. I looked to both guys and waited for someone to say something.

"I forgot to take my medicine!" Demetri blurted then hobbled out of the living room with his crutches. I glared at his escaping form then turned my attention to Alec.

He sighed and sat on the couch. "We need to talk."

"I don't like that phrase."

"Fine." Alec chuckled. "I need to ask you something."

Tense, I stood. I couldn't sit. Not if he was breaking up with me, not if he was ending the best thing that had ever happened to me. I knew things were going too well. My parents and I were finally talking, Demetri wasn't dead, thank God, and Alec and I were on our way toward bliss! It was only a few weeks until Christmas and I was hoping we would be able to spend our entire break together. I didn't want to spend it alone crying into a pint of ice cream.

"Nat, stop worrying." Alec pulled me down across his lap. I straddled him, but kept my body from touching his. "I love you." He kissed my lips and chuckled. "Seriously, you're stressing me out. Stop freaking."

I managed a tight smile. "So what is it?"

"We're going on vacation."

So not what I expected.

"Huh?"

"I imagined lots of screaming, jumping, and lots of kissing. *Huh* wasn't exactly on my list of answers." Alec flicked my nose and kissed my mouth. "We, as in you and I, are going on vacation before Christmas break."

"But we have like a week and a half of school and—"

"I've taken care of it."

"And my parents will flip out…"

"Already talked to them." Alec seemed bored with my excuses.

I glared. "I can't believe you would leave Demetri all by himself!"

Alec threw his head back and laughed. "Okay, first of all, you have trust issues. Second, Demetri is a grown man."

"Thanks dude!" Demetri called from the kitchen.

I rolled my eyes.

"And…" Alec's hands moved to cup my backside,

pulling me closer against him. "I've managed to convince your parents that you deserve a few days away from all this craziness. Besides, I have to go to L.A. to take care of some stuff."

"But…" I had no argument.

"Your teachers are more than understanding. In fact I'm pretty sure they could care less if a straight A student skipped out before break. Demetri is going to go crash at your parents'. Bob is staying with him, even though he begged for Lloyd." He would beg for Lloyd, the less scary one. Jerk. "And we'll be back in time to have Christmas together."

I bit my lip and looked at Alec. "As a family?"

He nodded. "Your grandparents, your parents, Demetri, and myself. That is, if you'll have us."

I squealed with excitement. "When do we leave?"

"Tonight." He checked his watch. "You have exactly an hour to pack."

I scrambled off his lap and nearly fell to the floor.

"Easy, Nat. I want to get you there in one piece."

I saluted just as Demetri hobbled back into the living room. Alec looked at me and then made some lame excuse about making sure he had everything he needed.

"So…" Demetri plopped onto the couch and motioned for me to join him.

"So." I repeated.

"My brother."

"Your brother."

"Are you really just going to repeat everything I say?"

"You almost died," I whispered.

Demetri sighed then put his arm around me. "I think I liked it better when you were repeating after me, Nat." I released a shuddering breath and looked at his face. He licked his lips. "Nat, I'm happy for you guys. I can't say that it doesn't suck, but I knew. Damn, I knew the minute you guys looked at each other. What can I say? I'm a selfish bastard. I knew what I was doing, Nat. Even if you didn't know your own feelings."

"But I love you!"

Demetri laughed. "Aw, Nat. I know, but it's not the same kind of love you feel for Alec. Believe me, I've felt that love before, and that wasn't it."

"Before?"

He nodded. A shadow fell across his features. "Once, and she died. I think in a way you reminded me of her. I was trying to fix things, by not really fixing them, Nat."

I leaned my head against his shoulder. "So what do we do now?"

"You mean other than make noises so my brother thinks I'm totally making out with you?"

I pinched him.

"Or that." He winced. "We stay friends, and you keep me far, far away from parties and alcohol-induced stupidity."

"We can always put one of those dog collars on you and press the shock button when you act stupid or make a bad choice."

Demetri threw his head back and laughed. "Kinky, I like it."

"Who's kinky?" Alec growled as he came around the corner.

"Your *fiancée*."

"We aren't—" I felt myself flush red. "We aren't engaged. It was just pretend." I assured them both and myself.

Alec said nothing, but Demetri grinned like a fool. "Yeah okay, Nat. You just keep telling yourself that you won't be marrying this one over here the minute he asks you."

I felt my cheeks heat even more! Glancing away I offered a nervous laugh and felt my treacherous heart jump at the thought. I was only eighteen for crying out loud!

"We good?" Demetri grabbed my hand in his.

I squeezed. "We're good."

"Love you, Nat."

I leaned over and kissed his cheek. "I love you, too."

Alec lifted an eyebrow.

I rolled my eyes. "Fine, I'm going to go pack!"

Alec followed me outside. The minute the door closed he pushed me up against it. "I can't wait to be alone with you."

I giggled as he kissed my neck and squeezed me against his hard body. "Finally, all mine."

"All yours." I hungrily searched for his mouth as he lifted me into his arms. Wrapping my legs around his body, I hung onto his neck and went about proving to him exactly how much of me he had.

Epilogue

"Merry Christmas!" I shouted, suddenly feeling like the girl jumping out of the giant present! Only I was jumping up and down and clapping my hands. After much convincing, Demetri and Alec both agreed to dress up as Santa and hand out gifts to the family. My little cousins decided to visit. They were twelve and fourteen. Both girls. And both avid fans of AD2.

"Ho, Ho, Ho," Demetri said very unconvincingly as he glared in my direction then tossed the girls presents. "My tummy is a rumbling like a bowl full of jelly."

I wrote the script.

Pretty sure they both hate me right now.

"I feel warm and cozy," Alec added, shaking his head. "But you know what will make me feel better, Santa?"

Demetri smirked, once a pervert always a pervert. "What, Santa?"

"A song."

The adults knew what was going on, as did I. We all clapped happily while Demetri and Alec grabbed their guitars and sat on the couch.

As the music started up, my cousins narrowed their eyes.

And then as both boys began to sing, I walked over and pulled off the beards and hats.

I've never heard girls squeal so loud in my life.

"Baby, I see your smile, it lights the sky, it makes me high with… Love is so deep, and feelings are strong. I need to feel close so I can carry on."

Then Alec's voice crooned, *"My Christmas star, I'll follow you far away. Far away. I'll be where you are, just promise me that you'll stay. Stay."*

They harmonized together, and I have to admit I was just as starstruck as my cousins. In fact, I was ready to pull out my cell phone and swing it back and forth in the air like a concert goer.

So many things had changed since my trip with Alec. We'd bonded more than I could ever imagine. He showed me all his favorite spots and even took me into the studio so he could start recording his acoustic album. Which Demetri finally gave him the green light on, considering he was going to be in rehab.

Demetri called us every day and every day my parents begged Alec to adopt both of them so they would be a part of the family, which I found alarming considering I was dating Alec. The parents who seemed not to care less about kids now had three. And it was awesome.

They weren't even staying at their own house during Christmas. My parents made up rooms for them, even though Alec was a little irritated that he couldn't sleep in my bed.

But my dad gave him the look, so he backed off and promised he'd sneak in later.

If anyone would have told me that my boring life would turn into what I was currently watching — two rock stars serenading my family on Christmas — I would have laughed. But I guess that's what makes life special. It's unexpected. Scary as hell. But in the end, totally worth it.

Pull

A Seaside Novel #2

Add evil.

Malicious.

Manipulative.

And crazy. To all of Nat's attributes.

Somehow she convinced her old boss that not only would it bring lots of business into Seaside Taffy, but having a legit rock star singing on the street would be almost like a tourist attraction.

I was not amused.

And I am still not amused.

Not when I'm driving to an actual job in a Mercedes that cost more than the building the taffy is sold in.

Nor when I get out of the car, grab my bucket — yes, there is an actual taffy bucket — and plop myself on the corner of the street.

People gather around. They expect me to sing the jingle. I want to kill myself. Why didn't I die in that accident?

"Seaside Taffy," I began. My voice cracked. It hasn't

cracked since I was five. Again, I want to die. *"Loads of fun, in your tummy. Yum, yum, yum."* I swear I can feel Bob snickering from twenty feet away. *"Ice cream, taffy, treats galore! Don't forget to stop at our store!"* I gave a dramatic bow.

I expected applause, or at least some sort of acknowledgement that I did just give the best performance of my life.

What did I get? One solitary clap. One person. I cringed thinking of the pity clap. It was the type of applause every performer dreads hearing. Swearing, I turned around. It was a little girl. She was five, by the way.

"Want some taffy?"

I held out a piece of taffy and the mom suddenly looks horrified like I planned to lay a taffy trail all the way to my car in order to abduct her child.

They hurried away and I'm stuck again with a crowd of people trying to get around me while I shake my bucket. "Seaside Taffy!" I yelled louder this time and threw my hands out in the air. Might as well commit, since this was my hell for the next few months.

"Seaside Taffy!" I flailed my arms again and a piece of taffy flew out of my hand, right into the back of someone's head.

Great. Add assault to my record.

The person turned around and I was a little shocked, because to be honest, I thought I had hit some punk kid.

Not. The. Case.

"Seriously?" The girl stomped toward me, all five feet of her and glared. She was wearing a hat that said "The Best Taffy in the World" and an oversized sweater with leggings and boots.

"It slipped," I offered lamely.

She reached for my bucket. I jerked it out of her reach. "Nobody touches the bucket."

Wow. I was so ashamed of myself that I wanted to jump

into the bucket and hide. Was I really getting possessive over my bucket? Like some homeless man with his cart?

She reached for the bucket again.

I snapped. "What's your problem!"

"My problem?" she repeated, her eyebrows shot to the top of her forehead. Damn, she had pretty eyes.

I nodded. Words weren't really my thing since I was shamelessly checking her out.

"My problem…" She laughed bitterly. "Is that the minute your punk rocker self got into this town, our business has suffered, and you don't even take it seriously! And now you're working my corner!"

"Whoa!" I laughed. I couldn't help it. "I'm sorry. Your corner? What? Is this Pretty Woman or something?"

"Did you just call me a prostitute?"

Yes. Yes I did. "Nope, more like a call girl. Prostitutes don't dress like blind middle schoolers."

"Agh!" She swatted my bucket, making all the candy fall to the ground. Amused, I crossed my arms and watched the fire blaze in her eyes. Really, it was a pity she dressed so horribly, and that she was wearing that awful hat. Though, I guess my visor wasn't any better, but still. I made it look good.

"Just watch it."

Brawl alert. I almost expected people to start coming out of the alleys with toothpicks in their mouths and newspapers in their hands.

How the hell did I get stuck in a Broadway musical?

Since I was committing to the whole Seaside Taffy act, might as well commit to this one too. "Noted, Shop Girl. Noted. Now run along."

Her eyes widened, and for a second I was shocked at how pretty she was. With a grunt and a cute little curse, she stomped off across the street.

I waved in her direction and started the jingle all over again. This time really committing, by way of throwing in a few AD2 dance moves that I knew would likely land me in prison if I moved to hastily in the wrong direction.

Three hours later, I was seriously rethinking this whole job business. It started to rain shortly after my dancing began. No doubt people thought it was because of my inability to keep my hips from moving with the stupid candy bucket.

With a sigh I adjusted my visor and tried to protect the taffy bucket. If my only job was to sell taffy and get people into the store, I didn't want to be the one loser who got the taffy wet and single-handedly took down the longest running taffy store in the history of Seaside, Oregon.

Thankfully, Bob must have sensed my plight, or maybe he was tired of me texting him every two seconds asking him for an umbrella. I knew it was pathetic, and okay, maybe a little bit ridiculous, but I was beyond drenched.

My teeth were chattering, and I was giving everyone with two eyes an unobstructed view of my nipple ring through the wet t-shirt.

If the mom from earlier was to come by now, she'd be horrified. And I'd be put in prison.

Ah, prison. Such a pipe dream. At least it's warm there.

"You're getting the taffy wet," a female voice said behind me.

Slowly I turned around. It was the big-eyed girl from before. Only now she was wearing a slick rain coat and rain boots.

"Caught that did you?" I sneered. I wasn't sure why I was so irritated. Maybe it was the rain? Maybe it was withdrawals from drugs. But I was pissed that the same girl who verbally attacked me from earlier would not only come back for more, but would blatantly tell me something I already knew.

"I'm not stupid," I said, shaking my head while still trying to shield the bucket with my body.

"You sure about that?" she asked, folding her arms.

"Did you seriously come back out here in the rain just to challenge my intelligence?"

"That depends." Her lips turned upward into a shadow of a smile.

Fine. I'll bite. "On what, Sweetheart?"

"Are you going to stand in the rain or move two feet and stand underneath the overhang?"

Shit. I looked up. Sure enough. There was a healthy overhang that could have been shielding me from the rain for the past two hours.

I shrugged, feigning nonchalance. "I like the rain."

She bit her lip and looked around. People walked around us with their umbrellas, all trying to duck into the shops until the rain stopped. I shivered in response and waited for her to say something.

"You chose the right place to be then."

If she only knew I had no choice whatsoever in the matter. "Yup, guess I did." Seriously. I was getting nowhere with this girl. All flirting genes apparently died in the car accident, while I was left very much alive — and very much a loser. What a bright future I had!

Author Note

I had so much fun writing this book. I think every author says this when they are done with a huge project, but there are so many people to thank that it would take pages for me to actually get through the thank you's, and by then you'd be wanting to throw your e-reader, so I'll start with the most important.

I thank God every day for allowing me to live my dream! It is because of Him that I'm even able to do what I do.

Laura Heritage. Editor extraordinaire. You are not only an amazing editor, but a fantastic writer and a wonderful friend. Thank you for believing in this project and helping to make it a reality.

Stephanie Taylor, Editor-in-Chief of Astraea Press and my publisher when I'm not doing a self published project like this one. Thank you for not only allowing me the freedom to do something crazy like self publish a book, but supporting me in the process and walking me through it. I don't know many publishers that would stand by and do that. I'm constantly in awe of you!

Thanks to my family and my sexy husband for putting up with me when I ignore everything but my computer for hours on end.

And finally, thank you to my readers. I love you guys so much! If you haven't already, add me on Facebook and Twitter and check out my website: www.rachelvandyken.com. As always, if you liked the book write a review. If you hated it, write a review. I love to hear the good and yes, even the bad.

Other books by Rachel Van Dyken

Every Girl Does It
Compromising Kessen
Savage Winter
The Parting Gift
Divine Uprising
Ruin

Renwick House
The Ugly Duckling Debutante
The Seduction of Sebastian St. James
The Redemption of Lord Rawlings
The Devil Duke Takes A Bride
An Unlikely Alliance

Wallflower Trilogy
Waltzing With the Wallflower
Beguiling Bridget
Taming Wilde

London Fairy Tales
Upon A Midnight Dream
Whispered Music
The Wolf's Pursuit

Seaside Novels
Pull
Shatter
Forever
Fall

from Forever Romance

The Bet

The Wager

Elect

Elite

Coming Soon:

Toxic

Shame

Irresistible Terms

When Ash Falls

Reign of the Lion

Alexander King

Entice

The Gamble

About the Author

Rachel Van Dyken is the USA Today Bestselling author of regency and contemporary romances. When she's not writing you can find her drinking coffee at Starbucks and plotting her next book while watching The Bachelor.

She keeps her home in Idaho with her Husband and their snoring Boxer, Sir Winston Churchill. She loves to hear from readers! You can follow her writing journey at www.rachelvandykenauthor.com.

Rachel Van Dyken Books